LOST SISTER

LOST SISTER

Jean Ryan

iUniverse, Inc.
New York Lincoln Shanghai

Lost Sister

Copyright © 2005 by Jean Ryan

iUniverse books may be ordered through booksellers or by contacting:

iUniverse
2021 Pine Lake Road, Suite 100
Lincoln, NE 68512
www.iuniverse.com
1-800-Authors (1-800-288-4677)

Cover photo courtesy of FreeStockPhotos.com

ISBN-13: 978-0-595-36651-4 (pbk)
ISBN-13: 978-0-595-81073-4 (ebk)
ISBN-10: 0-595-36651-1 (pbk)
ISBN-10: 0-595-81073-X (ebk)

Printed in the United States of America

For my sisters,
Jill, Joan and especially Jane

ONE

At the age of two she was wearing glasses, light blue frames with butterflies on the corners. Behind the thick lenses her eyes were enormous, and when she peered up at people on the street, they stopped and beamed at her; they couldn't help it. That wispy blonde hair. Those glasses.

So now she's in Virginia. I look at the photo on the postcard: a curving road, a field of yellow flowers, slate blue mountains in the distance, then turn the card over and read her words again. "It's hot here. The frogs are noisy at night. Lots of bugs too—I just counted 14 daddy longlegs on the ceiling. I have a job. Maybe just for the summer though. The kitchen is pink!"

This, as usual, is all the information she offers and I stand in the hallway trying to piece together her life. She forgot to include her address, though the postmark tells me that she's living in or near a town called Burkes Pond. She must be renting a cabin, something cheap and poorly made, on the edge of a lake. Her job is seasonal, dependent on tourists or vacationers. Maybe she's working at a roadside restaurant, one of those old snack bars strung with yellow light bulbs and mired in the sweet reek of fried food; families, barefoot and sunburned, swarm the place at dusk, jamming the battered picnic tables. Or maybe she's got a job at the boat rental, filling up gas cans, handing out red and white flotation cushions.

I walk down the hall and into my bedroom, a small rectangle barely big enough for the furniture: a mahogany double bed and dresser my Aunt Rose left me, a bedside table and a stuffed blue chair, occupied as usual by Murphy, my

16-year-old yellow tomcat. I pet his broad head a couple times, which brings on his staticky purr, and then I walk over to the corkboard on the wall and tack this latest postcard, photo side down, next to the others she's sent me. I collect these cards: I use them to track her, to fix her in time.

At the top of the corkboard are my two favorite pictures of Bett, the first taken just after she got her glasses. She is standing next to our green Plymouth station wagon and Barbara has a hand on either side of her head, keeping her face to the camera; I am there too, squinting, one foot hooked behind the other. She is still unsteady, and her legs, in red corduroy pants with snaps on the inseams, are braced apart, her arms lifted for extra balance. She is grinning, as she always was back then; her joy was instinctive, a natural, boundless response to being alive.

In the other photo she is wearing a two-piece, faded blue swimsuit and leaping ahead of a wave. She is four years old. Her golden hair is caught in the wind and she is shrieking with laughter. There she is, arms up, knee cocked, forever out-running the Gulf of Mexico.

When Barbara saw the postcards she started to cry. "Why do you do that? Pin them up like that, with her pictures on top. It's sad, Lorrie. It's like a shrine. It's like a missing person poster."

Her words startled me, because I knew they were true. I've been pursuing my younger sister for most of my life, even before she left home. There will never be enough clues in these cards she sends. They tell me where she is, but who, at this point, can find her?

Behind me Murphy stretches and groans. His groans sound human. He doesn't even meow like a cat. He opens his mouth and says, "Buk? Buk-buk?" Like a chicken.

He came to me by way of a friend who joined the Peace Corps and had to leave him behind. I wasn't thrilled at the idea of adopting him—I wanted a kit-ten, some sweet little thing that would race up the side of the bed, tuck itself under my chin and fall asleep. Murphy was nine years old and overweight. He had a broken fang and his ears were scarred and tattered at the tips. He didn't want much, just his food and a soft chair and permission to follow me around. He didn't twine around my legs, or ram his head into my hand, demanding to be petted. He didn't even cry to go out; he simply sat in front of the door waiting to be noticed, and if I didn't take heed, he would start to pick the threshold, very gently. It didn't take long to love him.

I bend down and kiss his head—it smells dusty—and his paws stretch and crimp. "Who's my boy?" I murmur, and he looks up at me in sleepy confusion, his upper lip caught for a moment on what's left of his fang. A bead of drool slides down his chin.

"Who's my beautiful boy?"

I check my watch again. It's 1:40 pm, which gives me ten minutes to get ready for work—more than enough time. Unlike most people, I dress down for my job, in jeans and sneakers and spotted T-shirts—only when I've managed to stain something is it suitable for work.

Some days I tell myself that a lucky chain of events brought me to cooking, that a mysterious and knowing force directed me away from the tidy corporate world and into the fun house of kitchen work.

And there are other days, more and more of them, when I look at my life squarely and find, not serendipity, but sabotage. That's when I see, with stunning clarity, each wrong turn I've made, and how much these blunders and bargains have cost me.

I should have stuck, in the first place, with science. As a child I was enthralled with shows that took me underwater: Flipper, Sea Hunt, Voyage to the Bottom of the Sea. I wanted to live in a world of chattering dolphins and singing whales; I wanted to search for giant squid with eyes as wide as dinner plates. "I'm going to do what they do," I announced to my mother one evening. We were watching a Jacques Cousteau special. Jacques had hold of a sea turtle and his crew—four skinny men—were cutting away the fishing net it was trapped in. My mother, snuggled into the sofa, sipped her scotch and nodded. She was happy, smoking cigarettes and watching TV; my father, who wouldn't permit these pleasures, was away on business.

Anything that slid through water, even through a mud puddle, captivated me, and I took to carrying a plastic bucket wherever I went, coming home with my catch of the day: silver minnows, velvety tadpoles, yellow-bellied newts. These I tried to nurture in a fish bowl on my bedside table, but they never lasted very long, especially the spry minnows, whose wizened bodies I'd find on the hardwood floor. One time I ordered a pair of seahorses through the mail. They were a disappointment from the start, a lot smaller than I imagined and not much fun to watch. For four days they clung to the scrap of seaweed they came with, and then they simply let go and died. They weren't, in the end, any better than sea monkeys.

Still I wasn't deterred. What I needed, I told my mother, was an aquarium, and, eyeing the latest casualty on my bedroom floor, she agreed. The next day she cashed in her green stamps and bought me a starter tank with all the accessories, and instead of scooping my pets out of puddles and ditches I began to buy them.

I still have that aquarium, and two others. That's what my dream has amounted to: three fish tanks in my livingroom.

Where would I be now if I had stayed true to this first love? Navigating the Amazon? Anchored off the coast of Figi? What would I be doing at this very moment if, 14 years ago, I had held my course and majored in biology? Instead, panicking over the math, I veered off into English literature. Wrong turn number one.

I take off my sweatpants and pull on the jeans I wore yesterday, then open my dresser and pull out a clean T-shirt. That's one of the compensations of cooking, not having to spend a ton of money on clothes. I don't have to fuss with makeup either; I work behind a swinging door and no one but the staff sees me.

I pause in front of the mirror and smooth back my short hair with my hands. My hair gets a lot of attention, mostly because I'm 32 and it's white. Ten years ago, when I noticed the first silver streaks, I was more curious than anything: if my hair was going, what else was? Since then I haven't given it much thought. People seems to like my hair, though that's not the reason I don't color it. The truth is, I can't be bothered, can't imagine having to worry about my roots and whether they're showing.

I lift my purse off the the doorknob and turn to Murphy.

"Okay, Murph. It's time."

He gets to his feet and carefully lowers his haunches to the floor. I follow his yellow bulk as he walks, head down, out the bedroom, through the kitchen and utility room, to the back door. He breaks my heart, this cat.

It's a sunny afternoon, surprisingly warm for the end of May. Locking the door, I smell the neighbor's creeping jasmine. Fat black bees hum in the red trumpet-shaped flowers that hang above my head. Vines have mobbed this place. You can't even see the fence anymore, just a cool blue wall of morning glory.

Though the rent is nearly half my income, I'm lucky to be here. Not many people in Berkeley get to live in a cottage, and this one, trimmed in flowers, is perfect. Just big enough for one person, or a couple, but only if they've learned to live like a pair of old slippers, side by side in quiet agreement. Rita and I never made it that far, which is why her leaving was such a relief.

The house in front of my cottage is occupied by Joel and Sasha, a free-spirited pair who grow marijuana among the tomato plants in our backyard. There is a three-story home next door and a set of apartments behind us, but people here respect this sort of enterprise and kindly look the other way.

Joel, who paints murals, is standing in his kitchen as I walk past the house. He lifts his beer and grins at me through the window, and I wave back. He is a slight man in his late 20s with green eyes and a gorgeous jaw. He dyes his hair platinum, wears neon-colored T-shirts and likes to sing, often in the garden as he trims his pot plants. Sasha is an ardent cyclist; today she's pedaling through the east bay hills, training for a race in Salinas next week. While not as good-looking as Joel, Sasha is the picture of fitness; I like the veins in her forearms, and I never get tired of gazing at her sinewy legs.

In the driveway, two strips of concrete with grass in the middle, sits their battered Volkswagen van. It's plastered with pleas: Save Mono Lake, Think Green, Buy Organic, Protect Your Local Planet. I don't have a car, or a license to drive one. At 16, having failed the road test twice, I blew my nerve; now I can't even think about trying again without breaking into a sweat.

Fortunately the restaurant is only four blocks away. Reaching the corner I turn onto Telegraph Avenue and the world is suddenly filled with cars and motion. On either side of the street people are taking care of business: walking dogs down the gum-studded sidewalk, shoving wet laundry into the dryers at Bing Wong's, pushing shopping carts through the Co-op parking lot. An elderly woman, her face mottled and shrunken, sits on a milk crate and holds out her hand. Coming toward me are three Hare Krishna, bald and equally ugly; then a tall black man who is talking to himself with great enthusiasm, his arms a blur of gestures. Next comes a Hindu woman in a hurry. She brushes by me, her eyes dark with worry; I look at the red dot on her forehead and feel as though I've just been warned—or cursed.

I don't see Zee's bicycle when I come around the side of the restaurant. Maybe she got a ride? No, Ann assures me, her voice exultant.

"Zee called an hour ago. She hurt her foot and can't walk. Or so she says," Ann adds, arching an eyebrow.

Shit. I grab a menu to see how much work I have to do; without Zee I'll have to prep the pantry station as well as saute. The salads aren't bad: Caesar, of course; mixed greens with a roasted shallot vinaigrette; butter lettuce with gorgonzola. Looking at the first courses I see that I have to clean mussels, slice prosciutto and make some kind of soup. Oh no. There are five pastas tonight and one of them has calamari in it.

I look up from the menu and glare at Ann; satisfied, she turns away.

"Why didn't you call me?" I say.

She shrugs. "I didn't think about it."

Ann likes me, as well as she likes anyone. She's just mad at the world and her revenge is reflexive. She's not pretty, that's the main trouble. Her face is a long box, her eyes are a watery, bloodshot blue, and her mouth is a junkyard of crooked teeth. What she really wants to be is a concert pianist; she doesn't like to talk about this and I have no idea what's stopping her. I do know that she's a good broiler cook, though she hates every minute she spends here and never tires of telling me what "crap food" we make. Today she's especially spiteful and, taking another look at the menu, I see why: one of the appetizers is fritto misto.

Robert, our bright-eyed, boyish pastry chef, has taken off his apron and is scraping the dried dough from his butcher block. While he works only four hours a day and could easily wash a case of lettuce, I don't bother to ask him: he won't. I don't blame him, in fact I admire his boundaries. Usually. Right now I can't even look at him.

I throw a pan of shallots in the oven and start slicing through heads of romaine. The lettuce is muddier than usual and in a few minutes my cutting board is smudged and gritty. And the quality isn't good either—there's no heart to speak of, just tough dark green leaves. Molly won't be happy about this, though it's probably her fault: I bet she forgot to pay the produce bill; either that or she sent them a bad check. Our paychecks bounce all the time, which is why we race each other to the bank; if we don't make it there before the funds run out we have to go back and tell Molly, who feigns surprise and remorse, then unlocks her desk drawer and pulls out some cash. I was stunned the first time this happened, and embarrassed for Molly, but now it's just tedious.

The water in the bus tub is dark brown—I'll have to rinse this stuff three times. At least I don't have to dry it by hand. Someone had the clever idea of buying a used washing machine; we just dump in the wet lettuce and turn on the spin cycle. You can only use it for romaine though, the other greens won't hold up. My anger mounts as I think about the flimsy butter lettuce and how long that'll take me; and the dressings, the soup, the pasta prep, not to mention the five pounds of calamari. For a minute I think about asking Molly to take if off the menu, but I know the pained look she'll give me and what she'll say: "Oh Lorrie, I wish I could, but the menus are *already printed*"—like that three bucks she spends at the copy place is such a big investment.

I look out the back door and see Juan watering the garden. Juan lives behind the restaurant, in an apartment owned by Molly. In exchange for rent he tends the garden, breaks down boxes, washes dishes and runs errands. On days when he's not feeling like a kept man, he can be charmed into helping me clean fish, chop parsley, dice onions. This doesn't happen often and it won't happen today. I can tell by the stubborn set of his shoulders, by the way his legs are planted, that my feminine wiles will be of no use.

Well I'm not making a pureed soup, that's for sure; and they're getting yesterday's crostini; and if I have to make salads all night I'm premixing the Caesar dressing and grating the Parmesan ahead of time.

There are a few small rewards: Zee squeezed lemon juice last night, we have four quarts of bolognese in the freezer, the faucet next to the stove has been fixed and we don't have any reservations until 6:45.

I grasp another squid, cut off the tentacles and squeeze out the soft white guts, then slide my finger into the slick tube and drag out the quill. And this is nothing compared to some of the things I do here. Last month, for instance, we had what they call the "Unmentionables Dinner," a ritual we practice once a year to amuse a few ruthless chefs. I think it benefits something, certainly not the animals. I couldn't bring myself to pluck the starlings so they made me peel turkey testicles.

The only civilized part of my workday comes at 4:45 when the cooks and waiters sit down to dinner. We're supposed to discuss the specials, which we prepare for this purpose, but after the first five minutes the conversation dilates and we end up talking about movies, or the concert program at the Greek theater, or a sublet someone heard about, or current airfare to Italy. Our wait staff is an accomplished lot, one a professional photographer, another a published author. None of us intended to work in a restaurant and we all believe we'll find a way out.

It's a night like many others. The start is slow, just a handful of walk-ins before the predictable 7 to 8 flurry, then a lull that nobody trusts. Sure enough we get hit again just after 9—a play or movie must have ended. For a while I manage fine, sprinting between the stove and salad station, keeping track of my tickets, but then they start streaming in and before I know it I'm buried. Ann, seeing this, barks out the orders and I just keep my head down and make them. At one point Paul, one of our newer waiters, tells me he needs a frutti di mare without scallops and an alfredo without garlic. "Write it down!" I hiss, shoving the ticket at him. He makes a note on the order and eases it back to me and I snatch it from his hand. The worst moment comes when he tells me he dropped a pasta carbonara. "Great," I say. "Fucking great. That helps a lot." He blanches and flees the kitchen and I hurl another saute pan onto the stove.

By 9:45 every table is eating and aside from plating a few desserts and putting things away my job is over. I walk over to the grill station and thank Ann for calling out the orders. Happy to be leaving soon, she gives me a snaggle-toothed smile and says she knows what it's like, working without a pantry cook. The floor in front of the deep fryer is splattered with grease and she's pushing a bar towel across the area with her foot. Ann's had a bad night too; her apron is filthy, her bangs are sticking to her forehead, and there's a fresh burn on her forearm.

Andre walks up with half a bottle of Montepulciano and pours us each a glass. "79 covers," he says. He turns to Ann and clinks his glass against hers. "And 32 fritto mistos." He looks at her, cocks his head in sympathy. "Sorry. I wasn't trying to sell them."

"Everyone loves fried food," I say, picking up my wine.

Paul rounds the corner and, seeing me, pauses. Feigning interest in the flowers on the end of the bar, he plucks off a few dead blossoms.

I walk over to him and place my hand on his arm. "Paul. I'm sorry for snapping at you."

"It's okay." He turns from the flowers and looks at me and I notice what long lashes he has. "I'm sorry about dropping that pasta."

Every night it's the same. The rush ends and we all emerge, as if from the same cage, dazed and grateful, our hearts swollen with forgiveness. I give his arm a squeeze and head back into the kitchen.

At two minutes after ten, a breathless young couple shows up at our locked door, tapping on the glass, pleading to be fed, and naturally Molly lets them in. What they want of course is pasta—I just dumped both pots of water.

There's no fog cover tonight and the air is chilly. Telegraph Avenue is quiet now, with only a few cars going by. I walk quickly, not because I'm afraid of being out at night, simply because I want to get home. I don't fear being assaulted in this city. Berkeley is home to the homeless, a haven for lost souls. The free-loving 60s still resonate, and while petty theft is common enough, real criminals can get no purchase here.

Murphy is waiting on the steps. He hoists himself up when he sees me and lays a paw against the door.

"Hi sweetie," I whisper, petting his back, which he arches in compliance. His fur isn't very soft anymore; like old upholstery it's showing wear.

Right away I pour myself another glass of wine and collapse on the sofa. On my clothes I can smell the foods I made tonight, my fingers reek of garlic. Murphy doesn't mind; he settles in beside me and gazes at my face. I love sitting here in the soft glow of the aquariums, Murphy purring, the pumps humming. Hypnotized by the movements of the fish, I lull myself into a stupor.

When I have finished my wine there is nothing to do but go to bed. Shifting Murphy, I rise from the sofa, my legs weak and rubbery. It's not good to be on your feet for so long. I'll probably get varicose veins.

I am so tired that even brushing my teeth is a chore. Accomplishing that, I wash up at the sink—no way could I manage a shower—and make my way to the bedroom. Buttoning my pajamas I study the new postcard from Bett. Virginia. A pond. A pink kitchen.

Murphy, considerate as always, lies down at the foot of the bed and I climb in and pull up the covers. A breeze comes through the window and I hear wind chimes. I don't like chimes, not at night. That disembodied music, that tinkling in the dark. It makes me feel lonely.

It's 2:30 in the morning in Virginia. I see Bett, unable to sleep, leaving her cabin and walking through tall wet grass down to the pond. The crickets are shrill and constant. A television flickers in a nearby window. When she reaches the mucky bank small green frogs jump into the water. She wraps her arms around herself and looks out over the pond. A zigzag of moonlight slides across the black surface. The cry of a loon carries over the water; she tries but can't see it. For several moments she stands there, her jeans soaked with dew, and then she turns around, heads for the yellow light of her porch.

TWO

I awake before dawn, my neck twisted awkwardly, my face pressed into the mattress. Do other people do this, torture themselves in their sleep? I roll onto my back and in slow waves the pain recedes.

My pajamas are damp with sweat. I was having a bad dream, struggling to lock a door while someone was pushing on it. I've had this dream several times and I never find out who's trying to get me. For some people sleep is a pleasure—Rita loved her nightlife—but I'd just as soon bypass mine. Maybe they'll make a pill one day, the equivalent of eight restful hours.

Once in a while I have an erotic dream and even those are disturbing. The thing is, you have no choice in the dreamworld. You fall asleep and you keep on falling, til you find yourself in a murky carnival from which there is no escape. Nothing makes sense and yet you believe, fooled anew each night of your life. It's monstrous, really, the way we are bullied in our sleep, the things we are forced to do, the people we employ without permission. And who knows if our dreams are private? In a realm where consciousness meets no limits, where anything can happen, might we be dreaming someone else's dream? A shared tub, that's what it feels like to me. Dirty bathwater.

Morning, naturally, feels like rescue, and it's always been my favorite time. For several minutes I lie in the dark and let my life find me. It's Saturday. The Ashby flea market. Shopping at the Green Earth. Work. Will Zee be there? A sore foot—that's probably good for at least two nights.

Murphy's warm weight is pulling on the covers. I nudge him with my toes and he stops snoring. A bird chirps, inciting others; they're as eager as I am for daybreak. Birds confound me. Why, for instance, don't we see them die? Shouldn't they be plummeting to earth left and right? And where do they go at night? And when it rains? They must be there, dozens in a single tree, lurking right before your eyes, like those hidden figures in children's picture puzzles.

Murphy groans; I feel his hindquarters stretch and shiver.

"Hey, Murph," I whisper.

"Buk?" he says, raising his head. "Buk?"

He always gets up with me, though I suspect he doesn't always want to. I turn back the covers and get to my feet and Murphy hits the floor with a soft thud. We walk through the dim rooms to the door and he picks his way down the steps, cautiously sniffing the air.

I like the whole coffee ritual, grinding the beans, dousing the grounds, warming my hands on the cup. I look forward to my morning French roast as much as I do my evening wine. These, truth be told, are the high points of my day, these equal doses of caffeine and alcohol. So far the three of us are getting along fine.

Sipping my coffee I study my fish, checking for signs of illness. Ever ravenous, they swim toward me, the trusty platys, the nimble tetras, the spooky see-through catfish. There's a lot involved in keeping them alive, and even healthy fish don't live all that long. Every week I have to vacuum the tanks and change out some of the water, and the plants need trimming all the time. I bend forward for a closer look and my four angelfish slide into view. One thing about tropical fish, you can't make eye contact with them. Their eyes are foil circles, yielding nothing at all.

I flip back the cover on the guppy tank and peer down at the fry. I used to let them take their chances in the floating weeds, but the steady attrition began to horrify me, so now I keep them in a plastic nursery til they are big enough to repel their predatory relatives. Look around you, look anywhere. There's no end to what needs saving.

After tending to the fish it's time to feed Murphy. I open the fridge, pull out a ribeye Ann overcooked last night and slice a third of it into thin squares. The vet warns against this kind of indulgence, claiming that Murphy, given his age and weight, should be on a strict dryfood diet. The idea appalls me. To force those hard pellets on Murphy every day of his life, to withhold his greatest pleasure, to deny him his ancestry: the taste of the kill. No. He is my beast and I will feed him what he loves. I slip real food to my fish too—minced clams, pink bits of salmon—because wouldn't they also go insane with misery, sucking down the same old flakes everyday?

As soon as the hot water hits my hair the shower is filled with the smell of green-lipped mussels. In my hair, on my skin, under my nails, I take my work home with me. Sometimes, tossing my T-shirt into the hamper, I wonder how many baneful organisms are clinging to it. I think about the knives and cutting boards that don't get washed enough, the food that sits out a little too long, the rusted can opener; and then I consider the exposed cut on my finger (a Bandaid is too risky) and the way Ann was coughing last week (cooks work when they're sick—no one wants to hear this but it's true), and what I figure is: diners are a lot sturdier than they imagine.

I'm halfway through toweling off when the phone rings. It's Barbara, I can tell.

"Lorrie?"

"Hi!"

"Are you busy?"

"No."

As usual, she gets right to the point. "Have you heard from Bett?"

"Yeah, just yesterday." I wrap the towel around myself and walk into the bedroom.

"I can't believe she moved again. And why Virginia? What was wrong with Tennessee?"

These questions are rhetorical and Barbara knows it. Bett has been on the move ever since she left Vermont, at age 17, with that creep Russell. Colorado was their first stop, some commune outside of Boulder; six months later they headed south, to Taos, where, fortunately, Russell drove his truck into a large pine tree and died on the spot. After that Bett moved to Lubbock and lived with his mother, but a few months later she sent me a postcard from Little Rock, telling me how much she liked it, and since then she's moved five times—that I know of. Now she has run out of land and will have to start heading in the other direction.

"Who knows?" I tell her, pulling a shirt off its hanger. "Oh—do you have her address?"

"Yes," Barbara sighs. "It's a P.O. box, of course. Wait a sec." She puts the phone down and I hear her quick steps walking away. I see her, tall and pretty, moving across the hardwood floors of her home. Barbara, being the oldest, had first pick of the gene pool, and she took the best of both my parents: my father's height, my mother's beauty. A moment later she's back on the line. "It's P.O. Box 54, Burkes Pond. The zip code's 24326. I can't find it on the map."

"It's gotta be there, Barb. I'll look it up in my atlas."

"The place she's staying in sounds awful—she said it was full of bugs."

"Did she tell you what she's doing for work?"

"This is what her card said: 'Hi. I'm living on a lake. It's pretty here but it's hot. I have spiders on my ceiling. I have a dog—he walked into the kitchen last week and now I'm feeding him. I have to go wash out the boats now. I'll write again soon. Your favorite sister, Bett.'"

I laugh. "That's the way she signed mine."

"What does she mean about washing the boats?"

"I guess she has a job keeping the boats clean. Probably those small aluminum ones."

"Oh Lorrie," she says softly.

"I know, but if she's happy what does it matter?"

"You really think she's *happy*?"

"Maybe" I say. "I don't know, Barbara, I wish I did."

Barbara always does this, asks me questions I can't answer. She wants certainty, resolution. Growing up she kept her clothes clean, her room tidy, her dolls lined up, and aside from a brief, reckless detour in high school—short skirts, bad boys—she has lived a sensible life, garnering whatever permits and possessions she deemed necessary. After graduating from UVM she moved to Connecticut, became a respiratory therapist and married a doctor. Open the door to her colonial home and you find two well-behaved children, one quiet husband and no clutter. When she is not securing that area she is busy teaching people how to breathe, something she herself has no time for.

"What about mom?" I ask. "Have you heard from her?"

"Not lately. I called her a few weeks ago and she seemed fine, except for the joint pain, her shoulders mostly. I told her she needs to take up yoga—like she'd ever do that."

I grin into the phone. My mother disdains any kind of exercise; her idea of breakfast is coffee and a cigarette. Thrice divorced and tired of the cold, she gave up on marriage as well as Vermont and moved to a trailer park in Florida, where she lives in a double-wide surrounded by vinyl geraniums and Astroturf. "A slice of heaven," she told me. I visited her there once. We spent all five days hunched over her kitchen table, drinking instant coffee or boxed wine and working on one of those giant jigsaw puzzles, a harbor at sunset. "Ah ha!" my mother kept saying as she seized a piece of boat or seagull and tucked it into place.

"What about you?" I say. "How's life in Connecticut?"

"Well, we've had two trips to the ER in one week. Jonathan fell off his bike and needed six stitches in his palm; he can't do any chores so he's thrilled. Alison had to have a tetanus shot—she got nipped by a colt." Barbara chuckles. "She doesn't want to be a vet anymore."

"Wow, what a week. You must be a wreck."

"Oh, I'm used to it. And Jack is a calming influence—nothing ruffles him, you know."

"And you?"

"I'm fine," she says. "Battling a little rash, but no real complaints."

Barbara has been "battling a little rash," off and on, since she was a teenager. Doctors haven't been able to agree on the diagnosis or the cause, and nothing they've given her has helped. I took two semesters of psychology in college, enough to realize that Barbara's problems can't be cured with ointments, and I've told her as much. Whether or not she agrees with this is of no consequence. The one time I suggested she find a therapist she frowned and shook her head. "They're all quacks. And besides, dwelling on that stuff only makes it worse." There's no point in bringing the subject up again, and if you know anything about Barbara, you know what I mean.

"What's new with you?" she asks, and I can hear the hope in her voice. Barbara wishes I'd get out of cooking; she says there's no future in it and she's right. A month ago I told her how much I like the UC Berkeley campus—the mythic cedars, the lovely old buildings—and she got all excited, told me I should go to the Office of Human Resources and fill out an application, that big universities offer all kinds of employment. It's not a bad idea and I don't know why I haven't done it yet.

"Not much," I answer. "No stitches or horse bites, at any rate."

"Have you applied at the university yet?" she asks, unable to help herself.

"Not yet," I say, and then, because it's possible, "I'm going to do that next week. On Monday," I add, embellishing.

"You've got nothing to lose," she reminds me. And we continue this way for a couple more minutes, she urging, me hedging, until there's nothing left to say but goodbye. I don't mind; this is how Barbara loves people. I just wish I had news that would make her happy.

There's no fog again today and the yard is spangled with sun. Coming outside I am enveloped in the prosperity of nature, the chirping of birds, the fragrance of new growth. Berkeley is never too hot or too cold, and from palm trees to pine trees, from cactuses to violets, everything grows here. As if in celebration of this bounty, Joel and Sasha are making exuberant love, and so common is this occurrence that I'm neither startled nor embarrassed as I pass beneath their bedroom window. Their ardor reassures me; I've come to depend on it.

After eight years I still find this city enchanting. It's the daring, the whimsy—you don't find it anywhere else. Students and workers, the poor and the wealthy, everyone contributes to the fun. The house across the street is painted like a ladybug, orange with shiny black spots, steel antennas coming out of the roof, wire eyelashes springing from the twin upper windows. There are homes that mimic boats, and trucks restored as homes, and charming bantam bungalows you'd swear belong to elves. Best of all are the yards, brimming with fuchsias and rhododendrons, graced with arbors and archways, birdbaths and statues; and all the vegetable gardens, blithely planted in front yards, the pole beans and cherry tomatoes dangling over picket fences, friendly as you please.

I walk past these neighborhoods to Shattuck Avenue, a long street hemmed with stores and harassed with cars, and then south to Ashby, an even busier stretch. At the intersection of these streets is the BART parking lot, where every weekend an assortment of vendors, the shady alongside the honest, try to sell their goods. There are Indians offering incense, Asians peddling toiletries, black men trading antiques, students dumping books, lesbians pushing jewelry. The whole edgy world can be found in this quarter acre, and I've gotten into the habit of coming here on Saturday mornings, to browse the crowd as well as the merchandise. There are treasures to be had, though I usually have to dig to find them. It's the small comforts I'm after—a soft flannel shirt, a sturdy spatula, a paperback novel. Today I talk myself out of a bonsai plant—only because I don't want to carry it home—and then I turn my back on a woman who wants to charge me $5 for a battered copy of Madame Bovary. After a while I get tired of rummaging through heaps of clothes and books, and I slip through a hole and out onto the sidewalk. Cars are passing in front of me. I've never explored this fringe part of Berkeley and, mildly curious, I cross the street and head west down Ashby.

I'm wasting my time, that's clear right away. There's no whimsy here, just graffiti and mingy apartments and liquor stores hiding behind bars. I'm about to turn around when I glance down a side street and see a child reading on the curb. I soften at the sight of her, at the capacity of children to lose themselves in smaller worlds, for there are boys on bikes racing past her, and a television blasting in a house behind her, and a Rottweiler wrapped around a tree, barking itself senseless. Something in the child's pose, in the way she's hunched over her book, beckons me and I start walking toward her. Coming closer I see the blue glasses, the blonde tangle of curls. My stomach leaps. For one lunatic moment I think I'm looking at Bett. Her fair skin. Her red cheeks. Her overbite. I stop and stare, and when she finally looks at me, her forehead rumpling just like Bett's, it's all I can do not to rush up and hug her.

"What are you reading?" I say. I can feel my heart beating in my ears.

Sheets of light slide across her glasses as she appraises me. She looks about eight years old.

"The Boxcar Children," she says, showing me the cover. "It's the one where they save the animals."

"Who are the Boxcar Children?" I ask, stalling.

"They used to live in a boxcar," she explains with exaggerated patience. "But now they live with their grandfather and they solve mysteries."

"Look," she says, pointing to a yellow balloon high above us. I can see her thrill as she watches it lurch in the wind, and then I see the scar on her chin and I remember Bett's scar, the one she got from sliding into a swimming pool backward and splitting her chin on the cement.

She doesn't mind when I sit down beside her; in fact she's pleased, though she tries not to show it. If she were older, even by a year, she might not allow this intrusion, she might dismiss me with a scornful glance; but I can see she's not done with childhood, has not yet lost that hopeful curiosity.

Her name is Ginger, she tells me, "like the movie star." This throws me. "Ginger Rogers?" I ask. She shakes her head. "Ginger from Gilligan's Island. The movie star." And that's not all. She has a sister called Margarita—named after her mother's favorite drink.

I ask which house is hers and she points to the one behind us, the one with the blaring TV. Someone is watching a game show. There are two large clay pots on the porch; a dingy white cat is languishing in one and the other holds a dead ficus. In the skeleton of its branches a bald, naked Barbie hangs by one arm. I look at the grease-spotted driveway, the litter caught in the shrubs, the packed dirt yard studded with yellow weeds and I can understand how the people inside might name their daughter after a character in a TV show.

In her expressions, in the line of her jaw, in the way her upper lip edges over the lower, I keep seeing Bett. It's the most private kind of fun, unwarranted and perfectly harmless, like the pleasure you take in seeing an acquaintance about whom you've just had an intimate dream: that false familiarity, that foolish delight.

The television audience gives a raucous cheer. I frown at the open window behind us and then look back at Ginger. The green plaid dress she's wearing is much too big for her; the hem has fallen in a couple places and there's a rip alongside the zipper. She isn't wearing shoes and the soles of her feet are black with dirt. I scan her arms and legs, checking for bruises. She's too thin, I know that.

"Are your parents home?" I ask.

"My *mother* is," she says. "She doesn't feel good so she's laying down." She reaches for her hair, twirls the ends with her index finger.

"Does she have a job?"

Ginger looks at the Rottweiler across the street who has stopped barking and is now sitting in exhausted silence; he can't even lie down, there's so little chain left.

"She has a box," Ginger says, shifting her gaze back to me, "with little make-ups in it. She gets money if she sells them."

I have a hunch this doesn't happen very often.

"What kind of job does your father have?"

Ginger shrugs. "He doesn't really have a *job,*" she says, her voice rising on the word, making it sound like a question. "He fixes things. He fixes cars. Toasters too."

I look at her lips, pursed for a second just like Bett's, and I nod slowly, absorbing what she's told me. "It's good to be able to fix things."

We fall silent for a moment. I cast around for another question, a way to sit here a little longer. In the pages of her book I see a paper with gold stars pasted on the top.

"Is that yours?" I ask, my voice rich with awe.

Ginger nods quickly and pulls out the paper.

"It's for spelling," she says, showing me. "I got every word right."

"Wow," I breathe.

She glances at me, suspicious, and then looks back at the paper and starts to explain. "My teacher, Mrs. Beck, she says the words and we write them down and then she grades our papers, and only me and Daisy spelled all the words right."

"You must like school," I say.

"I love school," she tells me, her forehead wrinkling with the fervency of this declaration.

"I bet you get lots of those stars."

"Lots," she says, tilting her head and looking at me over her glasses.

I think of Bett, who hated school, who disdained any kind of structured activity. She had no use for stars or medals; she didn't need that kind of validation.

However much Ginger resembles Bett, her personality is altogether different. She's very serious. I can't imagine her slipping Oreos behind her glasses and waiting for the teacher to notice. The things Bett got away with! Not through guile—

she simply wanted to entertain. And people sensed this, they let her disarm them. Barbara and I couldn't figure it out, how she invited trouble and never got into it. Most sisters would have been jealous; I guess she charmed us too.

In temperament Ginger seems more like me. A ferocious nail-biter, for one thing; I bet she goes to pieces over the slightest setback. And those gold stars she aims for. I edge another look at the ratty yard, the pile of tires alongside the garage. Why does she bother? Who in that house would demand such effort?

Again she fiddles with hair, spinning the golden strands near her temple into a knot. I want to give her something, some mitigating treat, and I notice the book in her hands, its worn edges and broken spine.

"I have some books," I tell her. "I can bring them to you if you want."

Ginger's eyes widen behind her glasses. "Do you have The Bears Upstairs?"

I shake my head. "No. But I have Black Beauty—it's about a horse, and Charlotte's Web—that's about a spider and a pig."

She grimaces. "I don't like spiders."

"You'll like this one. She's a very nice spider."

Ginger frowns, considering the offer. "Okay," she says. "You can bring them to me."

I tell her I'll come by tomorrow, and that my name is Lorrie and it's been a pleasure talking with her. She grins and looks at her feet.

I stand up and regard the dog, still hunched beside the tree.

"I'm going to unwind him," I say, beginning to cross the street.

"You can't," Ginger says. "He'll bite you."

And she's right. As soon as I reach the opposite curb the dog gets to its feet and begins to snarl. The fur on its back is standing up. "Good boy," I murmur, "good boy." It's no use. I walk back over to Ginger and say goodbye.

When I reach the end of the block I turn my head and see them, the child and the dog. They are watching me leave them behind.

THREE

On the way back home I stop at the Green Earth, a natural food mecca that smells like oats and vitamins and takes up half a city block. As usual the aisles are clogged with shoppers and it takes me thirty minutes to purchase a Mexican papaya, a bunch of broccoli, two pounds of brown rice and a bag of pumpkin seeds. You can't find any animal products here, and despite the crowd I enjoy myself in this blood-free zone: how restful it must be, living on greens and grains, no gristle or gore left over. Last week I was in the frozen food section of a super-market and I saw a package of quail, four tiny bodies huddled together, and all I could think was: *murder*. After five years of complicity, of severing squid and skewering shrimp, of cleaving pork ribs and boning chicken thighs, something in me is starting to recoil. The change is gradual now, but one day it will be com-plete. One day I'll be eating a ham sandwich and my throat will close in refusal. Waiting at the checkstand it occurs to me that I'm running out of time, that I had better find another line of work while I still have the choice.

Sasha is outside working on her bike when I come up the walk. She's wearing a red halter top and a pair of white shorts. Her body is as lean as her bike and I can see each one of her ribs as she bends over the derailleur. As always, I look at her legs, baffled by their economy.

"Hi," she says, glancing up.

"Hi. Going for a ride?"

"Grizzly Peak."

That's one of her favorite routes and naturally one of the most arduous in the area. She loves pedaling up those treacherous hills, trying each time to shave off a few more minutes. Sasha is a stage racer and the hill climbing part is what she's best at. I haven't known many real athletes and after two years of living next to Sasha I am still amazed by this unremitting need she has to conquer herself. I can't understand how a life can be pared down this far: to a bike, a road and a stopwatch. But then, who can account for passion? And it must be a relief, it must be a like a religion. Sasha worships all the great goddesses of cycling. In the bedroom she shares with Joel is a picture of her highest deity, a cyclist named Connie Young, the reigning world champion of sprint racing.

I watch her adjust the brakes, gripping and releasing the levers, turning the screwdriver ever so slightly. She is consumed by the task, her face so devout, so patient, she might be working on a fine violin.

Sasha has three bicycles, each one fully insured, which she keeps in the garage and protects with a sophisticated alarm system. I don't know what metal they make bikes out of these days, but judging from the weird lightness, the staggering cost, I think it's mined in outer space.

"The flowers look nice," she says, pointing to the purple and white alyssum I planted along the walk.

"Thanks." I'm pleased, and surprised, that she noticed. "There's lots of lettuce and green onions in the backyard. Take some—I can't eat it all."

"Okay," Sasha says, bending back over the bike. A perfect line of white scalp bisects her thick dark hair.

"I met the cutest little girl this morning." Already I feel foolish—why should this interest anyone else?

"Oh yeah?" Sasha says. She taps her screwdriver against her palm, ponders something on the bike.

"She looks…she reminded me of my sister. When she was a kid, I mean." The words, pointless, trail off.

"That's neat," Sasha says. "Oh." She glances up at me and her hair falls across her cheek. "Rita came by. She left a note."

"Thanks." I turn and head down the walk. Sure enough there's a folded piece of paper sticking out from under the doormat. I bend down and pick it up, immediately recognizing Rita's flamboyant script. Lorrie! I miss you! What are you doing tomorrow? Call me. Kisses, Rita.

You'd never know from the messages Rita leaves me that we broke up nearly a year ago and that she's involved with someone else—a big blonde named Sheree. Rita's loyalty is fierce and constant, and I've wondered if she isn't trying to make amends for having lost interest in me last spring. Now that she doesn't have to sleep with me, I can hardly fend her off.

I don't mind her devotion, it's flattering after all. Nor am I jealous of the women she dates. I fell out of love with Rita six weeks after she moved out (sometimes it happens that way, sometimes love cooperates; you're asleep, or on the phone, or washing dishes, and love, weary and unwanted, leaves without a scene). But it is disconcerting, how fast she installed this friendship. I'm not even sure how much it means to me, what I'd do without her. I don't get the chance to find out.

We lived together for four years, my longest running relationship. It seems I spent my twenties in a sort of training, each romance a little more successful than the previous. Before Rita there was Kris (two and a half years), and before her there was Elizabeth (just over a year), and before her there was Tony (a matter of months)—actually I never fell in love with Tony; she was more an introduction than a love affair.

It's hard to calculate the duration of a romance. The starting point can be roughly determined, but the finish is tricky; you have to keep backtracking. Rita and I were finished long before she left. Long before she feigned exhaustion to keep me on my side of the bed. We were doomed at some point in our third year, maybe the morning she walked into the livingroom and announced that the aquariums, which she once delighted in, made the house smell like a swamp and did we really need three of them; or it might have started earlier, with some mannerism of mine that she suddenly couldn't abide. When love turns to treason nothing can be done, and I don't hold Rita's desertion against her. Well, not anymore.

Now, like I said, she's my biggest fan, and the only person, other than my sisters, who knows my soft spots. I can see her nodding when I tell her about Ginger and how much she reminds me of Bett. Have I heard from Bett, she'll ask, and I'll tell her about the postcard from Virginia, and she'll put her hand on my arm. "You miss her so much," she'll murmur, at which point I may start to cry.

I unlock my door and Murphy runs up the steps and rushes inside. He does this now and then, hides in the ivy as I come up the walk, then ambushes me. Nothing cheers me more: my big yellow tom, broken-fanged and stiff-hipped, still game at the age of fifteen.

The answering machine on the kitchen counter is blinking and I punch the play button. It's Molly, telling me that Zee is still having problems with her foot so Suzanne will be helping out. "Perfect," I sigh, pulling my groceries out of the bag. Suzanne is Molly's niece, a sullen 16-year-old who comes in with her arms folded across her chest and her face deadset against us (she is bribed of course; Ann told me what Molly pays her and it makes me want to a smack a saute pan against my forehead). Despite having worked with me at least a dozen times, she refuses to acquire any familiarity with the pantry station and must be told every time to wash the romaine, juice the lemons, grate the parm. Naturally she moves at the speed of a loris, and by 7:05 tonight we'll be done for. I can see it now, Suzanne languidly tossing salads, ignoring the jam of tickets, my constant pleas. Her blonde hair will be hanging into the mixing bowl, the floor will be littered with lettuce and the wait staff will turn into a lynch mob.

Obviously I need to go in at least an hour early; since it's already past noon I don't have much time to prepare myself. I open the fridge and look wistfully at the bottle of wine, but I know better. A glass of wine would make me drowsy, and even less inclined to go to work.

Murphy saunters across the kitchen, tail raised, the tip waving slowly, like a question. At the threshold of the bedroom he stops and looks over his shoulder at me.

"You've got an hour," I advise, and he slips from view. I swear this cat understands everything I say.

I put the broccoli in the crisper and the lumpy green papaya on the counter, and for a couple minutes I stand at the sink eating pumpkin seeds and studying the spider plant that hangs from a ceiling hook. Although I feed and water it regularly, it's not doing well; maybe it's demoralized by the unbridled plant life outside the window, all those savage vines thriving despite their bugs and bad dirt. I look at the rest of my collection, fruits mostly, pits and seeds I've coaxed into plants: a lanky avocado, a reluctant lemon, a date palm that may or may not make it. Mired in jelly jars, leaning toward the light, they look, just now, like captives, stuck in this window the rest of their unnatural lives.

Maybe this is what finally sent Rita packing, this knack I have for seeing the dark side of things. She once told me I could find tragedy in a rainbow. In the beginning I think my dour observations amused her, but as time went on she refused to chuckle at them and instead would frown and change the subject. A few times we argued about it, her accusing me of self-indulgent wallowing and me protesting that I couldn't pretend to be someone I wasn't, and where was the harm anyway—I was getting along just fine. Maybe our demise started earlier than I suspect, the seeds taking root in the dark, sprouting, perhaps, on our very first date. Such conjecture isn't very useful, though I am comforted by the idea that my life, to an unknowable extent, is out of my hands.

Defending his naptime, Murphy is curled up tight in the bedroom chair. This pose means he doesn't want to be disturbed and I resist the urge to pet his plump gold side. In the corner next to the chair is my makeshift bookcase—a stack of orange crates. I kneel down to look in the bottom carton, filled with children's classics I've collected over the years, most in excellent condition and many still wearing their original dust jackets: Tom and Huck lounging on a river bank, a steamboat in the distance; Hans Brinker gliding down a canal on his new silver skates; Black Beauty gazing at me, her brown eyes wet with trust. This last volume has charming illustrations and nice thick pages, their edges shaded the color of coffee. I hesitate, unsure now about lending them to an eight-year-old. I could take off the jackets, I guess. I could caution Ginger about washing her hands first, and not bending back the spines. I could show her the right way to hold these books. And in no time at all I could probably destroy her interest in reading them.

Hell. What am I doing with children's books? When was the last time I read one of these? I pull out Black Beauty and The Black Stallion, and then, considering Ginger's neighborhood, I reach for the Swiss Family Robinson. The crate above contains a few paperback classics and from these I take The Incredible Journey and, as promised, Charlotte's Web. It occurs to me that some of these books might be too advanced for Ginger's reading level—I'll read them aloud. The thought, for a moment, undoes me, and I sit back on my heels, remembering the times I read to Bett, the way she'd interrupt, argue with the author; the way her mind raced ahead of the story. Too soon she outgrew my help and was reading, prodigiously, on her own. "She's smart, that one," my grandmother warned us. "Too smart for her own good."

I put the books on my bed and walk over to the corkboard. It's remarkable, unsettling, how much Ginger looks like Bett. The broad face, the curving forehead. My father, with a grin on his face, used to call her "The Ugly Duckling," a term Bett still uses, breezily, to describe herself. What a master he was at cruelty, his blows so persuasive, so offhand, you didn't even know you were hurt.

I move to the dresser and pick up a photograph of my mother taken a couple months ago, I guess by a neighbor. She is sitting in a deckchair, a cigarette in one hand, a bright orange drink in the other. Under her straw sunhat she is smiling— I'm glad of that.

There was a time when I wanted to chase her down, make her pay, at least explain. Not anymore. Behind those sunglasses I can picture her steel-gray eyes and the fear they reflect. Let me be, they are saying. Please.

I've thrown out every photograph of my father, all except one, which I keep in a box on the floor of the closet. There is nothing significant about this picture; it is simply small enough to store easily. I don't why I keep it, or why, every couple years, I find myself studying it. Certainly it brings me no pleasure. Looking at my father is like touching a scar.

FOUR

If I have to work with Suzanne one more time I think I may do her harm. I knew she hadn't washed that lettuce properly and when the first Caesar she sent out last night came back, I wanted to put my hands around her scrawny white neck and choke the daylights out of her. It goes beyond being lazy; that kind of negligence borders on the sinister: you have to be heartless to care that little. I told her she needed to wash all the romaine again and to hurry up because it was already 6:30, and she narrowed her little pink eyes at me and flipped back her hair and I knew the night was only going to get worse. After that I think she was screwing up on purpose. Two of her tickets disappeared during the rush (I found them later, stuck to the bottom of the olive oil can), another salad came back (overdressed this time), and at 7:15 she informed me, with no apparent concern, that we were out of house vinaigrette. I was holding a bottle of Pernod over an order of sea scallops, and I stopped to stare at her.

"How much did you make?"

She lifted her hands, turned away. "I didn't make any."

Well you can imagine what I was thinking just then, the things I wanted to scream.

"Make a quart," I said, flaming the pan, "and go home."

I thought I handled myself pretty well, or maybe I just didn't have any fight left in me. It had been a bad night all around, starting with the dishwasher breaking down, again, swamping the kitchen so that we had to stumble around on lumpy wet towels all evening. And then the trouble with the fish order, which didn't arrive til 4:15 (when restaurants don't pay their bills on time, vendors have ways of getting back at them). The shellfish was fine, but I could stick my finger through the seabass they sent us.

"It's not bad," the driver assured me, "just soft."

I frowned at him. "Are you kidding me?"

He shrugged and reached for the box. "I'll take it back."

"Do you have anything else?" I asked, my voice softening. Maybe I could charm him out of a nice chunk of swordfish. "I need a special."

"I got sand dabs."

"Cleaned?"

He grinned. "No way."

"What else?"

"I got some squid." I shook my head.

"And snapper. That's it."

I grimaced. Snapper, that drab old standby, our Saturday night feature. Would Molly never learn?

But it's Sunday morning and I have two days off, and I'm going to try very hard not to think about the restaurant. I take my coffee into the backyard, where Joel is grooming his six marijuana plants, snipping off the larger leaves and bending back the tips to encourage the side shoots. They're nearly four feet tall now, and beginning to overtake the tomato plants alongside them. Joel is wearing only his pajama bottoms and I admire his strong smooth back as he ties down a branch with a strip of gardener's tape. Such perfect forms, he and Sasha. How gratifying it must be, how restful, to look like that. To stand before a mirror and find nothing wrong. To make love, without pause, in broad daylight.

He waves his scissors at me and grins. "Morning!"

"Good morning." I sit down on the redwood bench. "Think you've got all girls there?"

"Maybe. I think so." He points to a smaller plant at the end of the row. "Except that one, that might be a male." Joel steps back a minute, admiring them. "The heat's helping—weird, isn't it, this weather?"

"Yeah. It's supposed to be cooler tomorrow though."

"What are you up to today?" he asks.

"Well I'm meeting Rita for lunch, but before that I'm going to visit this little girl I met yesterday." Just saying this elates me.

Curious, he stops what he's doing and looks at me.

"How did you meet her?"

"I went to the flea market, and then I started walking down Ashby and I saw her sitting on the curb." I shake my head. "What a crummy part of town. Bars on the windows. Graffiti. Anyway, I'm going to give her some books to read."

Joel nods thoughtfully. "That's really nice of you."

"She got to me," I tell him. "The thing is, she looks just like my sister Bett, at that age."

"Bett," he says. "That's the one who lives in the south, right? Tennessee?"

I'm touched that he remembers this. Joel reminds me a little of my first love, a guileless boy named Timmy. Some boys are graced this way, with an innocence they never outgrow; oddly, you don't see it in girls.

"She lives in Virginia now," I tell him. And for several minutes we talk about Bett. I tell him the funny things, the candy she used to sneak out of the house in her wool stocking cap; the birds she let loose at the children's zoo; the time she stuffed potatoes up the exhaust pipe of our station wagon. Snipping leaves, tying branches, Joel laughs, and the world, for an instant, holds together, slides into perfection: the green row of plants, the steam coming off the sun-warmed fence; the peeling shutters and chalky clapboards; the bedroom curtains moving in the window; the khaki-colored snail headed for my pole beans; the clam shells under the picnic table, remnants of our Easter feast.

"Joel?" Sasha says from their bathroom window. "Where's the Fast Fuel I just bought?"

He looks up at her.

"I need it. I have to leave in twenty minutes."

"I don't know," he says. "Oh. It's still in the bag, in the livingroom." He turns to me, makes a face. "I don't know how she can drink that stuff."

Ginger is waiting for me in the same spot I left her, wearing the same green dress. I say hi and sit down beside her and she hugs her knees and grins at me. She has teeth like a doll, small and square and white, with slivers of space in between. I grin back, alarmed: has anyone ever looked at me with such patent delight?

It's probably close to 80 degrees and the air here is motionless. The cars, the dog on his chain, the crumpled cans on the lawn across the street, even the stunted sycamores look like they're waiting for something.

Ginger's hair is stuck to her forehead in tiny golden rings; it could stand to be washed, I notice, as could her nails, which are etched with crescents of dirt. Casually I ask what she ate for dinner last night and she tells me she had a cheese sandwich. "I made it myself," she adds, reaching for her hair.

"Oh," I say, all innocence. "Your mom lets you make your own dinner?"

Ginger nods vigorously. "She *likes* me to."

A black lab comes panting up to us. Tongue lolling, he sniffs our knees and jogs on. Ginger doesn't seem the least bit afraid of him; she's too busy eyeing the books I've brought. I hand them to her one at a time. "Can you read these?"

"Yes," she declares. "I can read one grade more than I am. Mrs. Beck said." She reaches for Black Beauty and her dress falls off the pale bone of her shoulder. Stomach clenching, I watch her rifle through the book to the first page.

"Chapter One," she announces. "My Early Home." She eyes me haughtily and turns back to the book. "The first place that I can well re…member, was a large pleasant…muh, meed—MEADOW, with a pond of clear water in it." She stops, hunches closer to the book and starts on the next sentence. She does fine til she gets to the word "plantation" and she's really stumped by "whilst."

"You know what?" I say. "I can read them to you. It'll be more fun." I pick up Charlotte's Web. "Let's start with this one, it's my favorite."

We look at the drawing: Fern and Wilbur gazing at Charlotte who hangs from the webbing around the title. Ginger wrinkles her nose. "I don't like spiders," she tells me again.

"This is a special spider," I promise her.

A teen-aged boy comes out of the house across the street, and ignoring the Rottweiller who jumps up hopefully, gets into a shabby Datsun in the driveway, starts the engine and turns on the radio, loud. I wait for him to back out of the drive but he just sits there, fouling the air with dark billows of exhaust. Ginger and I move farther down the curb, and raising my voice above the angry thumping music, I start reading about Fern Arable and her efforts to save Wilbur, the undersized pig. I keep expecting Ginger to break in, the way Bett always did, but she stays quiet. A couple times she taps my arm and asks me to read a sentence again, and when I do, she listens closely, nodding and smiling to herself. Just as I reach the end of chapter four, a woman drives up in an old yellow Ford Galaxie. Ginger and I watch as she swings out of the car, slams the door and heads for the house. She's a tall woman, rake-thin, with straggly red hair and long pasty legs. A pack of Kools sticks out of the front pocket of her fringed denim shorts. Halfway to the porch she glances over at us and her steps slow a fraction; I can see the doubt and confusion on her face. It looks like she might come over, ask who I am, but her desire to avoid us is stronger and with a warning scowl she turns her back and hurries to the front door.

"Is that your mom?" I say and Ginger nods.

"Is your father home?"

"No. He went on a trip. To L.A.," she adds, emphasizing the letters. "That's a city. It's not near here."

I look behind us at the livingroom window and imagine Ginger's mother behind the blinds, lighting up a Kool and squinting at us through the smoke.

"Maybe we should stop for now." I shut the book and place it on top of the others. Ginger gives me an anxious glance.

"I could come back some other day and we can read more."

"Tomorrow?" she says immediately.

I hesitate, afraid of her wide open need. I can't even go in a pet store, can't look those stranded creatures in the face.

"Sure," I say, my voice falsely cheerful. "Why don't you keep these here," I tell her, pointing to the books. "That way you can read them whenever you want." She beams at me as I get to my feet and I feel a surge of shame, like I'm leaving the books as a means of escape.

"See you later," I say, edging away.

"See you later," she echoes, waving hard and earnestly, like children do.

Maybe, after Bett, I have no reserves left, no space to harbor another soul. I don't think she ever knew the lengths I went to foster her. She was busy taking care of herself. What daring she showed, tossing aside rules, ignoring boundaries, fashioning a childhood she could move around in. Although she managed her schoolwork with ease, she often shunned it just for the fun of forging a good note: Dear Mrs. Drew, Bett didn't do her homework last night because her grandmother forgot to take her medicine and had to be rushed to the hospital. People loved that excess in her. Later, her tales became more extravagant, her maneuvers more evasive, and still no one thought to be concerned.

How did she do it? How did she manage to slip away while everyone was watching?

I get off the bus at University Avenue and walk three blocks to the Thai Garden restaurant. As usual I have to wait for Rita (she likes to make an entrance) and I spend a few minutes looking at the sculptures on the wall, frightening paper mache masks decorated with gold, lacquer and paste jewels. The one over my table has a green face and wild eyes and looks like a monkey gone mad. I sneer at it, in defiance, and turn to the giant wooden panel near the door, every inch of it filled with carving. Tilting my head, I try to identify one of the strange fish-like creatures, and Rita sweeps into the room, bright-eyed and breathless.

"Lorrie," she cries, stretching out her arms and bending down to give me a hug. "How *are* you? Have you been waiting long?" She drapes her purse over the back of her chair and sits down. "What time *is* it?"

"It's ten after one." I point to the green mask. "I don't get this art."

She glances up, nods in agreement. "It's pretty wild."

Rita looks great. She has a stylish new haircut (she's forever revising herself) and the peach-colored blouse she's wearing shows off her deep skin tone. Catching me admiring her, she flushes with pleasure. I can remember when that smile devastated me, and I think how odd it is that I can appraise her now with perfect calm, my desire a piece of lost luggage.

"We should order now," I tell her, opening my plastic menu, "before we get to talking."

Rita scans her menu, then pushes it across the table. "Chicken in green curry sauce," she says. "They make great curries here."

"I can't decide between shrimp fried rice or shrimp with Thai basil and chilies."

"You always get the rice," she says. "Try something new."

"Okay." I put my menu on top of hers and immediately a young Asian waiter appears at our table and, nodding and smiling, takes our order. Rita provides a good example by ordering green tea. I come close to considering this idea before asking the waiter for a glass of white wine: rarely do I surprise myself.

"He's sweet," Rita says, watching him hurry back to the kitchen.

"How was your morning? You were at the shop, weren't you?" Rita is a hair stylist; she has her own salon in north Berkeley.

"Good. I had a major triumph."

"What do you mean?"

"This 70-year-old woman came in and told me she wanted a perm. I asked her how long she'd been curling her hair and she said 40 years—can you imagine? So I talked her out of it. I gave her a wash and wear cut and she was thrilled."

"But you lost money, didn't you?"

"Sure, but the point is, I freed her." She looks at me askance, a guilty smile breaking over her face. "Also I'd just done two hennas and I was running out of time."

"Ah, now I see. You're lucky she liked it, you know. Has anyone ever burst into tears afterward?"

Rita laughs. "Well, not while they were still in the shop, thank god. And they do come back, most of them." She unwraps her knife and fork and spreads the paper napkin across her lap. "What about you. What's new? How's work?"

"Hideous. I didn't have Zee this weekend. She hurt her foot or something." I think of the mushy seabass, the soggy towels, Suzanne, and I realize I don't want to talk about any of it. There is no meaning, no weight in what I do; it's the same old slapstick every night, and I'm as tired of relating these silly tales as Rita must be of hearing them.

"I got a card from Bett—she moved to Virginia."

"Oh," Rita says softly, infusing the syllable with dismay and compassion. She knows all about Bett.

"She's living in a cabin on a lake." My gaze swings to the front window and the people passing by. "Naturally she's adopted a dog," I sigh, "some stray that walked into her kitchen."

"Did she get a phone?"

"I doubt it. I don't think she's had a phone since she lived in Little Rock. I asked her about it once and she said the ringing made her jump. I don't imagine she can afford one either."

Rita looks at me. I can see her mind working behind her deepset eyes. "How long has it been since you've seen her? Before we met, right?"

"Just before—five years ago."

"You need to see her," she says simply.

I pick at the tines on my fork. "I'm afraid to."

"That's why you need to."

Now she's done it. I feel the tears start to pool and I keep my head down.

"I know," I tell her.

"One of my clients is a travel agent. I'll find out how much it'll cost to fly there. What's the name of the town?"

"Burkes Pond." I look up then, straighten my shoulders. "I don't know what it's near."

"We'll figure it out," she says, putting her hand over mine. That's when I notice the tiny flowers she has painted on her fingernails—roses, daisies, petunias.

"Good god. How long did that take?"

"Aren't they *great?*" she cries, showing me the complete collection. "It didn't cost me a thing. I took it in trade. Two haircuts, one for each hand."

There it is, I think. Proof. A perfect illustration of the gulf between us.

The waiter arrives and places a stocky glass in front of me filled to the brim with wine. Rita gets her own little teapot and a ceramic cup with a blue dragon on it. He pours the steaming tea, swamp green with bits of leaves that eddy and settle in the bottom of the cup, and then he turns on his heel and heads for the kitchen.

"I'm starving," Rita announces. She has a tremendous appetite, and luckily a fast metabolism.

Tilting my head forward I bring the glass to my mouth. It's awful, way too sweet. I'm not disappointed, it's always awful.

Seconds later the waiter returns with our food. Rita takes a bite of a curry and, in her dramatic fashion, leans back, closes her eyes and moans enjoyment. My shrimp dish is equally delicious, though I manage to stay upright when I try it.

As we eat I tell Rita about Ginger, how I met her, how much she looks like Bett, what her neighborhood is like, my fears about her welfare.

"They left her alone?" Rita says.

"Apparently. No sign of a sitter. The mother's real rough-looking. Trailer trashy. Didn't even say hi to Ginger when she came home."

"Does Ginger have any siblings?"

I pause, remembering what Ginger told me.

"A sister, but I haven't seen her. You'll love this: her name is Margarita— mom's favorite drink. 'Ginger' comes from Gilligan's Island. The movie star."

Rita laughs. "Well that says it all." She swirls a piece of chicken through the sauce and brings it to her mouth. "What's she like? Ginger."

I take a sip of wine. "Serious. Loves to read. Loves school—she'll be starting fourth grade." I spear a shrimp, rest my fork on the plate. "She's nervous, though, high-strung. She bites her fingernails and fiddles with her hair. And she's thin." I get angry then, thinking about the dress she was wearing and the way it kept falling off her shoulders. "They had her in a dress about three sizes too big, and the zipper was ripped."

"You can't do anything about it," Rita cautions. "You're feeling this way because she reminds you of Bett. But she isn't Bett and you shouldn't get too attached."

"Too late," I say, reaching for my wine.

FIVE

People used to tell me that my father looked like a movie star; Burt Lancaster was the one they cited most. I admit he was a handsome man. I say "was" not because he's dead, but because I don't think about him. Rumor has it he's alive and well—makes no difference to me.

For good measure I changed my last name (not that I expect he'll come looking for me, but who knows). I never liked my original name anyway; it had a gravelly sound and no one could spell it. I wanted something simple and weightless, something I could slip on and walk away with. The trick to naming yourself is to do it quickly: too much deliberation and you're stuck with an investment. It took me about five minutes to come up with "Rivers," a pleasant word I plucked out of nature. No one has trouble with a name like Rivers, and saying it still gives me satisfaction.

The other thing people mentioned a lot was my father's brilliance. He was a doctor and our family enjoyed an undisputed status in the neighborhood thanks to his god-like powers. Every now and then an apologetic mother would arrive on our doorstep with her fussing, feverish child, and my father would dispense his winsome smile and lead them into his study from which they'd emerge 20 minutes later, the child hushed with reverence, clutching a lollipop, the mother thankful and thoroughly besotted. And that night, during dinner, my father would tell us what "a goddamn idiot" she was and how "cows like her" shouldn't be allowed to breed.

Looks meant a lot to my father. Even more than intellect, he prized perfect features and from early on we were all made aware of our individual defects (I was not allowed to wear socks with my Sunday school shoes as they made my unfortunate legs look even more stubby). Bett, however, with her thick glasses and wide face, got the brunt of his ridicule and how she managed it I'll never know. Barbara, aloof and clear-sighted, disdained my father and, as much as possible, removed herself from his presence. I, on the other hand, was fearful, ever anxious to appease him. But you could never tell what Bett was thinking, which might have been another thing my father resented about her.

What is burned deepest into my memory is the day he got rid of Bett's dog. I was eleven that year, Bett was eight. We had just moved to Texas, my father having decided to become partners with a former associate, a physician in Dallas who had opened a clinic and needed help with the growing client base. Missing the deep woods of Vermont, I didn't like the flat brown stretches of Texas, but soon enough I found compensations and spent my days scouring the desert for arrowheads and fossils.

In the same way she attracted people—especially those who were headed for trouble—Bett charmed every stray animal she encountered and it was not uncommon to see some hapless mutt trailing her home from school. Pets were forbidden at our house; this was a rule as stringent as all the others my father imposed and instinctively we didn't challenge it. But one day, when my father was out of town attending a medical conference, Bett met a dog she couldn't discourage, a cowed black and white spaniel with one glazed eye. My mother, in a rare moment of defiance, accepted responsibility, and for the next three days she and Bett worked on that dog, prying off ticks, cutting off matts, soaping and hosing its skinny frame. By the time my father returned the dog was presentable, if ugly, and both my mother and Bett were smitten with it. In a fight that lasted for hours my mother held her ground, and my father finally relented, on the condition that we keep the dog out of the house and out of his sight. My mother cut down one of the packing boxes, lined it with old blankets and tucked it into a corner of the garage, and that's where Heidi—Bett named her—spent her nights (Bett of course tried to join her there, but my father was a light sleeper).

There was something wrong with that dog, a part of her that couldn't be soothed, and by the end of the second week we all knew that things weren't working out. The problem was, she didn't want to be away from Bett, not ever. In the middle of the night she would start to whimper, and then I'd hear my father cursing, threatening to "shoot the damn thing." When Bett went to school, Heidi wanted to follow her; when we drove off in the car she would chase us down the street. My father said he'd never seen such a stupid animal, and my mother would edge a cold look at him and say, "You're all heart, you know that?" And from the back seat Bett would argue, "Heidi isn't stupid, she's just lonely." But the last straw came when my father found scratches on his freshly-painted back door. An uncompromising man, he liked to do things himself, not trusting the competence of others. He had painted all the trim on our house and had also put in his own lawn, his own mimosa trees and his own flagstone patio. Naturally we were terrified of damaging anything he created, and my mother knew when he showed her the back door that Heidi would have to go.

When Bett came home from school that day my father told her that they were going for a walk. "Heidi can come with us," he said, smiling. Seeing how calm he was made my stomach hurt: I'd gotten home before Bett and I knew about the door. Bett didn't trust him either, she knew he hated that dog, but of course she no choice. And maybe she was thinking this might be just another nature lesson—he was forever teaching us facts about the world we lived in.

I got on my bike and, keeping a distance, started to follow them down the drive and across the street, past the row of houses being built, past the mesquite trees and the giant clumps of cactus, all the way to the dry river bed and the rocky field beyond it. My father knew I was behind them; he didn't care, he liked an audience. They stopped at the edge of the river bed and I heard him tell Bett to pick up some stones. She began looking around, trying to choose carefully, probably thinking he was going to teach her something about these smooth white rocks, when he barked, "Just pick them up!" She knew then, and so did Heidi, who stopped dashing around them and crept over to Bett, lowering her haunches to the ground. My father bent down, reached for a stone, then threw it at Heidi, striking her in the side. She yelped and jumped to her feet.

"Throw your stones," he told Bett. "Throw them at her. You have to be the one to throw them."

She stood there, frozen. I couldn't see her face, just her gold hair, the edge of her glasses, but I could hear her. She was crying, pleading with him, saying no no no, til her voice was raw, til he shouted for her to do what he said, til he marched over to where she stood and there was nothing she could do but start throwing those stones. The dog, not understanding, kept coming back, running away and coming back, but losing ground each time, til she was across the river bed and running into the field, but still turning around, still stopping, still looking at Bett, who was sobbing and throwing those stones, not at the dog anymore, who was too far away, she was just throwing them, exhausting herself, while my father, delighted, shouted approval. "Good job," he kept saying, "good job!" And the dog got smaller and smaller, til all I could see was a dark spot in the parched field that stopped one last time and then disappeared.

SIX

There's nothing Murphy likes more than to wade through fresh compost. He's purring away, belly-deep in the fluffy mahogany dirt as I try to mix it into the garden.

"C'mon, Murph, that's enough," I say, nudging him out of the raised bed. He tries to hop back in and I block him with my arm. "No." He sits down, gives me an injured look, and then is distracted by a bird in the magnolia tree next to the cottage. Bits of compost cling to the gold fur on his chest and legs.

I plunge my spade deep into the dirt and heave it back up. "And you're not coming in the house like that."

Joel opens his back door and steps outside.

"You sound nuts, you know, talking to your cat."

I look over my shoulder at him and smile.

"What I want to know is, does he answer you? Can you hear him?"

"Yes and no," I say. "He answers through expression and body language. He's much too advanced for oral communication."

"Now I know you're nuts."

Joel's hair, the color of white gold, is still mussed from sleep. He is wearing a bright orange T-shirt and baggy grey sweatpants and in his hand is a small plastic bag of marijuana. He walks over to the pot plants and I see the logo on the back of his shirt: Yosemite Sam brandishing his oversized pistols.

The fog, which rolled back in last night, is just beginning to lift and patches of blue sky can be seen. It's going to be a perfect spring day.

"I'm glad the fog is back."

Joel nods. "Yeah, but the plants don't like it." He's right: the branches, which were spread wide in yesterday's heat, are tucked in now, making the plants look cold and hesitant. Joel walks down the row, bending close to inspect the tips, looking for early flowers, confirmation that he's not wasting his time.

"Hah!" he says after a moment. "We have a girl."

Skeptical, I put down my spade and walk over to him. "It's not even June yet." But when I peer at the tip he's pointing to, sure enough there are two tiny white stigmas poking out. Joel finds another set on the plant next to it and tells me we have to celebrate. He sits down at the picnic table and rolls a joint and we pass it back and forth as the sun burns off the last of the fog. Pete, our burly next-door neighbor, comes out onto his deck and waves down at us.

"Morning," he says.

"Morning!" we answer unison.

We like Pete. We don't even care that he built a deck off the second floor of his house and can see our backyard. He minds his own business and always mows our patch of lawn out front whenever he mows his own yard; he trims our hedges too. In return we look after his chihuahua, Thor, whenever he's out of town.

Pete settles into a deck chair with his mug of coffee and a newspaper and Joel stubs out the joint.

"Is Sasha here?" I ask.

"No, she left for Salinas at 5:00 this morning. She won't be back til Wednesday."

"How long is the course?"

"75 miles." He looks over at Murphy who is laying on the porch step, idly washing a paw.

"That's one big cat."

I nod, a little too long, and realize how stoned I am.

"Did you grow this?" I ask, pointing to the bag.

"Nah, I ran out. Had to buy it."

"It's good."

"Oh yeah."

We sit there a while without talking; it's another thing I like about Joel, how easy it is to share silences with him. A mockingbird flies out of the magnolia tree and Murphy, seeing it land on the fence, makes that weird chattering noise that cats make when they see something they'd like to kill. The bird aims an eye at Murphy and squawks right back. You can't intimidate a mockingbird. One time, walking down the street, I passed too close to a nest and a pair of them came out of nowhere, shrieking and flapping their wings in my face.

The bird flies off and my gaze moves on, finding, in the corner of the fence, a large spider web strung with dew. I stare at it a moment, and then, as if instructed, I get to my feet and approach the shimmering circle. Joel watches me and when he sees what I'm headed for he gets up too.

"Great spider," says Joel. We are standing a foot from the web and the spider is hanging head down in the center. It has a large black body with bright yellow markings; four legs are stretched out in front and four stretched back. The web is perfectly constructed, like ship's rigging, and the spider, waiting for a victim, looks proud and wonderfully evil.

"It's an orb weaver," I say.

"Are they poisonous?"

"Not to humans. But they kill their prey with one venomous bite. Then they eat them."

Joel, impressed, reflects on this and then says, "Let's help it. Let's find a bug."

"No thanks," I tell him, moving away. "I'm feeling too good to see something that horrible."

"You're right," Joel says and walks back over to the picnic table. "I have to get going anyway." He picks up the rolling papers and the bag of pot.

"Are you working today?"

"Yeah. Tommy'll be here in about ten minutes." Tommy is Joel's partner, a 25-year-old Asian with straight black hair that falls to the middle of his back. He is short, nice-looking and well-mannered—and clearly in love with Joel. It's a fruitless, enduring love, and Joel, if he notices, doesn't seem to mind.

"What are you working on?"

"A bank on Claremont. They want one of those old-timey pictures—lamp posts, carriages, people in hats." He makes a face.

"I saw the mural you did for Outfitters Inc—the snowboarders coming over the ridge? It's great, Joel. They look like they're flying right out of the wall. Everyone was stopping to look at it."

He smiles. "Yeah. I like that one too."

Tommy's good with paint, but Joel comes up with the designs and does most of the sketchwork. Sometimes he draws at the picnic table and I love watching his hand move over the paper, how quickly the lines turn into a picture. If I could draw like that I wouldn't be able to stop.

Joel goes inside and in a few minutes I hear Tommy's big white van pull up. I pick up my spade again and start mixing the pungent compost into the vegetable beds. I want to buy a gift for Bett, and I'd like to get my gardening done before I head downtown.

But what? What does she need? Everything, that's the problem. The last time I saw her, in that apartment in Little Rock, she didn't even have a cutting board, or a decent knife, or a non-stick skillet. She never was a practical shopper. I remember the last time I went shopping with her, it was the Christmas before she and Russell left for Colorado. She had about eight dollars to her name and she spent it on a set of fake fingernails and a poinsettia plant for my mother.

I wonder how she'd feel about opening a box of kitchen supplies. Would I embarrass her with gifts like that?

Maybe I should get her something to wear. A pretty blouse; a jacket. But I don't know her size, or what she likes, or if she cares at all about clothes.

Something for the dog, then. I know she cares about animals. I could go to that great pet store on College Avenue and buy a nice collar, a pretty leash.

No. Bett would never put her dog on a leash. Or live in a place where you had to.

Food? I could send her a gift box, one of those meat and cheese samplers from Hickory Farms. She used to love those little sausages my mother gave us for breakfast.

But what if she doesn't eat meat anymore? Maybe I should send her chocolates instead. She can't have given up sweets. Not Bett.

Or I could forget about Teflon skillets and clothes and candy and send her something she really needs—money. I could say it was a housewarming gift. But Bett would see right through that, and she would send it back.

I smooth the surface of the dirt, realizing I don't know anything about this sister I shared a room with; there are too many miles and years between us. But even when we were children, inhabiting that same precarious world, Bett kept her secrets, as if, way back then, she was fashioning her own myth.

When people ask if I had a happy childhood I say yes—the part of it I spent outside. That's where children go for solace. I think of Ginger sitting on her curb and how awful it must be to grow up in a place without woods and meadows.

In the winter Bett and I used to strip the boughs off pine trees and weave them into forts. The snow would fall down the back of our necks and our mittens would freeze and we'd have to stamp our feet against the cold, and still we hunkered inside those green walls. They were *ours*, those frozen oases; inside them, safe as unmapped treasure, we had power.

Barbara can't understand why Bett keeps moving from town to town, from cabins to trailers to rooms for rent. I know why: she's still building those forts, looking high and low for cover.

Books! What better present for Bett? There, waiting for me in the store window, is a three-volume set by Larry McMurtry. I know she'll like these tales of hard luck and small triumphs, and I buy the books the way I buy everything I'm sure of—without checking the price.

Once again Ginger is sitting on the curb bent over a book—*Charlotte's Web*, it turns out. At least she's wearing a new outfit, a faded purple dress with a large stain on the bodice. She eyes my backpack and I tell her I bought a present for my sister. Disappointed, she looks away.

"Do you like wearing dresses?" I ask.

"Yes," she says without hesitation.

This interests me. I hated being imprisoned in dresses when I young (in fact I still do) and I find it strange that any child would prefer them to T-shirts and blue jeans, though maybe, living in a place like this, it doesn't matter. I look at the feeble sycamores—who could climb those things?

There's no car in the driveway, no television blaring, and it occurs to me that Ginger's parents have left her alone again.

"Where are your folks?"

Ginger twirls a lock of hair. "My father's still gone—he's in *L.A.*" She likes saying L.A.

"And your mom?"

"She left."

"When will she be back?"

Ginger shrugs, picks at a scab on her knee. "*I* don't know. At dinnertime I think."

I look at the greasy driveway; the pile of tires in front of the garage; the bald Barbie in the ficus. The Rottweiller is still chained to the tree and I have the horrible thought that he is never free of it.

We could go to the cottage, I realize, my heart quickening. I could show her the fish, make her some lunch; I could read to her without having to shout or swallow exhaust.

But how wise is that? She's probably been told to stay here. I don't have permission to take this child several blocks from her home.

On the other hand, her parents aren't here to give me permission. They've left their eight-year-old alone; they do it all the time.

We'd be back in a couple hours. They wouldn't even know.

I grasp my knees and beam at Ginger. "Do you want to see my fish?"

"Yes," she declares, getting up quickly so I won't change my mind. I point to her feet. "You need to put some shoes on." She hands me the book, runs into the house and comes out a minute later with a pair of white sandals flapping on her feet.

"Can you walk in those okay?" I ask. Like the green dress, they're much too big for her. She assures me that she can, and then she takes my hand and off we go, easy as pie. Too easy.

"What's that one?" she asks, putting a grubby finger on the side of the aquarium.

"A neon tetra."

"What's that one?"

"A bleeding heart."

"*A bleeding heart?*" she echoes, bringing her face close to the tank, trying to see this gruesome phenomenon. She scrunches her forehead, purses her lips, and I see Bett.

"Give me your glasses a minute," I tell her. "They're covered with fingerprints."

Obediently she hands them over and for the first time I see her whole face, disarmed, helpless. No longer able to see the fish, she turns away from the tank and simply waits, her gaze suspended and peaceful.

She likes the sunken ship and the way the fish swim through the hole in its side. I tell her about the otters in Monterey Bay and how they wrap themselves in kelp before they fall asleep; and the sea turtles that swim through the green depths of the ocean, day and night, hundreds and hundreds of miles, to lay their eggs on the beaches they were born on.

"How do they find them?" she whispers.

"Nobody knows," I whisper back.

After that we settle on the sofa and I open Charlotte's Web and start on Chapter Five. Right away I discover that Ginger has been reading, quite successfully, on her own.

"SOME PIG!" she shouts when I get to the part where Charlotte leaves a message in her web. I look at her and laugh. "Have you read this whole book?"

She nods and then nudges my leg with the hard tip of her sandal. "Keep reading."

"Please," I remind her.

"Please," she says, reaching for her hair.

I read several more chapters and Ginger listens carefully, sometimes murmuring a sentence along with me. I'm amazed by her recall, the quickness of her mind, so reminiscent of Bett. Or maybe this is typical; maybe children, ignorant of their limits, acquire knowledge more easily than adults. I can only make guesses about children, having chosen to live a life without them.

"Are you hungry?" I say, closing the book.

Ginger frowns. "We're almost at the end—it's sad."

"I know, but my voice is tired. We'll finish it next time. C'mon, let's go find something to eat."

She follows me to the refrigerator and shakes her head at everything I point to. I don't blame her; there's not much here to tempt a child: a half bottle of wine, some milk that might be bad, a gooey wedge of gorgonzola, a tin of anchovies, a wilted bunch of arugula, broccoli, a few carrots. She wants to know what that big green thing is on the shelf and I tell her it's a papaya, from Mexico, and that she might like it. "I don't think so," she says, shaking her head decisively.

I open a cupboard and push aside the cans of tomato sauce and white beans and pumpkin filling.

"Ah ha!" I say, seizing a can of Campbell's soup. "Chicken with rice."

Ginger points at the jar of peanut butter. "We can have peanut butter and jelly sandwiches," she offers.

We look for some jelly; all I have is a small jar of peach chutney that's been in the fridge for at least three years.

"No *jelly*?" Ginger says, but she's even more disgusted when she finds out I don't have any white bread.

"Have you ever tried this?" I ask, showing her the loaf of rye.

She fold her arms across her chest. "Soup," she says.

I fold my arms across my chest and arch an eyebrow. She brings both hands to her mouth, grins.

"*Please.*"

Before we leave I show her the spider in the corner of the fence.

"Ewwwww," she says, taking a step back and reaching for my hand.

"It won't hurt you."

She eyes it, mistrustful. "It doesn't look like Charlotte."

"It not the same kind of spider." I circle the edge of the web with my finger. "Look how big the web is—that's a lot of work."

"It's silk," Ginger tells me.

"That's right. The silk comes out as a liquid and then it hardens right away—like cotton candy."

I start to tell her why spiders spin webs but that's where the facts start getting gruesome. Ginger's fears won't be dispelled by learning that spiders feed on the liquefied remains of the bugs they turn into mummies. So I lead her to a gentler part of the yard, my vegetable beds, and show her the peas, snug in their pods, and the row of baby corn plants. One day, I swear, they'll be six feet tall and sprouting corn on the cob. She looks at me over her glasses, not buying a word of it.

I tell Ginger that we should be heading back and she asks if she can see the fish one more time—a ploy, I know, but how can I refuse? She spends a couple minutes in front of each tank, delaying our departure with questions I can't answer: "Why do they call them angelfish?" "Do fish get tired of swimming?" Finally I put my hands on her shoulders and nudge her toward the door.

"Have you heard of the Steinhart Aquarium?" I ask her.

She shakes her head no.

"Well, all kinds of fish live there, thousands of them. Sharks, sting rays, octopuses. Turtles too. I'll take you there someday."

She gapes at me, absorbing the news in silence, in every atom of her being. Immediately she becomes docile and follows me out the door.

I have made a promise to a child. It's my second mistake today.

We stop at the end of the driveway to admire the ladybug house again and Ginger tells me that when she grows up she's going to live in a butterfly house, she's going to make the wings herself.

"What color?"

"Yellow," she says decisively. "And red. Them two."

"*Those* two."

"*Those* two," she repeats.

"Well I hope you'll invite me over because I'd really like to see it."

A few minutes later we come to the truck house—an old Ford pick-up, the bed of which has been turned into a Swiss chalet with gingerbread and mullioned windows and dainty flower boxes. Ginger wants a boost up so she can look inside and I tell her it's not polite to peek into people's windows. We walk on, discussing the advantages and disadvantages of living in a truck, and as we near Ginger's street I start to get nervous. What if Ginger's mother beat us home? What will I say to her?

Someday, Ginger is saying, she is going to show Margarita the truck house.

"How old is Margarita?"

"Five."

This surprises me; I assumed she was older than Ginger. An angry, truant teen.

"She lives in the hospital," Ginger explains. "There's something wrong with her heart."

Drugs, I think, picturing the mother's rawboned frame. Alcohol.

"When she gets better I'm going to show her the truck house. *And* the ladybug house."

"It must be hard," I murmur, "living in a hospital."

Ginger considers this a moment, then says, helpfully, "She's really good with her Etch-a-Sketch."

We reach Ginger's house and my heart kicks into my throat. There's a man in the driveway, and from the way Ginger reacts I know it's her father. Abruptly she lets go of my hand; I can feel her stiffen beside me. Shirtless, hunched behind the raised hood of his truck, he straightens up and stares at us. I can see each one of his ribs and a long scar than starts below his breastbone and ends somewhere below his belt. His hands are black with oil.

"Where *you* been?" he says, his voice snide, accusing.

"We took a walk," I say quickly, edging in front of Ginger. "I live nearby—I showed Ginger my tropical fish."

He rolls his eyes at this and turns back to the truck. I walk over to him. He has some kind of cyst on his shoulder; it sticks out like an egg.

"I'm Lorrie Rivers."

"Yeah, I know about you," he says, peering at the engine. "Why are you hanging around Ginger?"

I don't know how to answer this. I give him a false, bright smile and say: "Oh I'm just keeping her company. I've been reading to her."

He snorts. "Well I think it's weird." He picks up a long wrench and begins loosening a bolt. "Don't you have anything better to do?"

I watch the tendons moving in his forearm. How can I explain anything to this man?

"I'm sorry," I tell him. "I shouldn't have taken Ginger out of her yard without your permission. I'm very sorry." He keeps fiddling with the engine, refusing to look at me. "Next time," I add, "I'll ask you." He doesn't say a word, but I do get a slight nod out of him.

I walk back over to Ginger and say goodbye, assuring her that I'll be back soon.

"Tomorrow?" she wants to know. I glance at her father.

"Not tomorrow. The day after."

She frowns at this news and mutters okay, and I give her hand a squeeze and head back up the street. A few seconds later I turn around to wave but she's already gone inside. Away from him.

He gives me the creeps. That hard nub of a chin; the way his pants hang on his hip bones; the look on Ginger's face when she saw him: not quite fear; not hatred either, not yet. It was a look of dread.

What can be more dreadful than childhood? Old age, maybe. Either way, you're doomed to submission. Though at least when you're old no one wants to touch you.

Of course I suspect him.

SEVEN

Zee is back, and limping, which makes me feel bad for assuming she'd lied about her foot. She was jogging and hit a pothole. Her swollen ankle is wrapped in an ace bandage and though she's supposed to stay off it, she needs the money. Right now she's sitting on an overturned bucket shelling fava beans, splitting the big green pods with her thumb and dropping them into a bowl between her feet. As usual, she works quickly. Zee doesn't so much complete a task as she eliminates it, bringing herself one step closer to the day she will leave us again. That's her bargain. She gives us six months of hard work and we give her three months off. Tom, her carpenter boyfriend, negotiates the same terms. After slaving and saving for half a year, they hole up in their west Oakland studio where he writes poetry and she creates garden sculptures—unfathomable creatures begot from salvage yards. Nobody is waiting in line to buy these goods and I'm impressed that Zee and Tom have the heart to keep making them, arranging their lives around art that no one wants.

I toss some broken mussels into the trash and spill the good ones into a Tupperware container.

"Are you sure you're okay to work?"

"Oh yeah," Zee says. "I'll just sit down between tickets. It only gets bad if I stand for too long."

I look at her doubtfully. "We have an eight-top at 6:30 but not much after that. A few deuces."

"I'll be fine."

Zee, who just turned 40, has an unstoppable energy. She reminds me of a sparrow: quick dark eyes, sudden movements; no one can touch her speed when it comes to prep work. In less than 15 minutes she had all the lettuce cleaned, even with a bum foot.

"How was the romaine today?"

"Not great."

I shake my head and slice a rock cod into bite-size pieces. "I don't know why we can't just order the hearts."

This is an open invitation to deride Molly and her misguided ideas, a sport enjoyed by nearly everyone who works here, especially Ann. But Zee is different; she just shrugs and picks up another bean. She doesn't need the solace of mean-spirited gossip—she's only here on loan.

The doors swing open and Ann comes into the kitchen. Before I can say hi, she snaps:

"Are we out of towels?"

She has colored her hair again, violet this time, which makes her pale skin look even worse, and her bangs have been hacked off way too short. For all I know, this may be the latest European style (Ann is well-traveled and likes to correct me when I mispronounce names like Majorca), but the effect is frightening, especially under the fluorescent lights. I look back down at my cutting board.

"Yes," I tell her. "Molly's bringing some dish towels from her house."

Ann sighs in disgust. "We gotta up that fucking order. We run out every week." Then she turns and straight arms her way back through the door.

"She's going to be fun tonight," I murmur, and Zee chuckles noncommittally.

One advantage today is Juan. He strolled out of his apartment pleasantly drunk and after fixing the leaky faucet over the stove, volunteered to clean the shrimp. He is working next to the sink and singing along to a Spanish radio station, embellishing the songs with a variety of sound effects.

A black Mercedes rolls up behind the restaurant and Molly, with some effort, emerges from the driver's seat. She is a woman of ample proportions and her movements are slow and grand. Even her smile comes on gradually, in stages I like to watch: her mouth turning up, her crow's feet deepening, her chin sinking into her neck. When she is not smiling her face assumes an expression of vague contentment, which works like a shield, deflecting all censure and confrontation. I have never seen her angry.

"Hello all!" she says, coming through the door, her arms full of dishtowels and groceries. These she deposits on the salad table, then turns her benevolent gaze on us. I admire her blue silk jacket and how it sets off her blonde hair, which is pulled back from her face in that style worn by women of wealth and a certain age.

I thank her for the towels; Zee says hello; Juan lifts his knife and grins.

Molly looks down at Zee. "How is your poor foot?" she asks, her head tilted in sympathy.

"Better," Zee says up, standing up in proof.

"Well I hope so. Don't overdo it tonight." She turns to me. "I bought pasta. Four pounds of fettucine, three penne and three angelhair—you think that'll do it?"

"Plenty," I tell her.

"Good," she says, casting a suspicious eye on Juan as she passes through the kitchen.

I'm not thrilled about having to cook off dried pasta (Alberto, our pasta man, called in sick) but the rest of the prep isn't bad and with Juan helping we'll be ready ahead of time. At least that's the way it looks until he slices open his index finger cutting bread for crostini.

It's partly my fault. I shouldn't have given him the brand new serrated knife; I should have let one of the waiters cut those skinny baguettes into quarter-inch rounds.

I don't hear him yelp, probably because that's all he's been doing for the last hour. I don't notice he's hurt til I see him hunched over the sink with one of Molly's blue-striped towels wrapped around his hand.

I come up behind him and put my hand on his moist, meaty shoulder.

"Let me see."

He shakes his head. "No problemo."

"Juan, I have to see it." Not that I want to, believe me. Reluctantly he extends his hand and, wincing, I unwrap the towel and draw a sharp breath. It's a messy wound: his knuckle is split to the bone and half his fingernail is gone.

"Hold it up," I tell him. "Keep the towel tight."

I hurry through the swinging doors and Ann, who's yanking the skin off a monkfish, looks up.

"Juan cut himself."

"Bad?" she asks, intrigued.

"Bad enough."

Molly is presiding at her desk, a bulky antique in the front of the restaurant where she spends many serene hours turning her paperwork into a shambles.

"Juan cut himself," I tell her. "He needs stitches."

"Oh dear," she murmurs, an expression of polite concern passing over her face. "Who shall we send?" She looks out over the diningroom, makes a selection.

"Ask Paul. He can take my car." She hoists her enormous black satchel onto her lap and fishes for the keys, and I ask Paul if he wouldn't mind taking Juan to the hospital. Andre, our head waiter, takes it in stride, smoothly acquiring another waiter, as well as a dishwasher, with a single phone call. Having been with Molly since she started Elba, Andre is a master at damage control; I doubt we'd stay open without him.

Luckily it's a slow night and I am home by 10:30. The van is in the driveway, which is odd: Sasha wasn't due back til tomorrow. Walking under their bedroom window I hear organ music and stilted dialogue—Joel loves old horror movies— and I picture him and Sasha lounging in bed, their perfect bodies stretched side by side. A feeling gusts through me then, not quite loneliness, more a reminder of it: I am living without something I need.

There is Murphy, a gold statue on the dark steps. He gets up when he sees me and arches his spine.

"Murph," I whisper.

"Buk," he says.

There is a phone message, from Bett. My stomach jumps at the sound of her voice.

"Lorrie? Are you there?" Silence, then, "It's me. I'm at the store"—a chuckle—"buying dogfood." Another silence. "I'm fine. I like it here. They let me use the boats." A sigh. "I'll call you later, okay? Okay then—bye." A pause. "I just wanted to talk. Bye."

I play the message three more times. Is it my imagination or did her voice start to get quivery? "I just wanted to talk." Why? Is something wrong? You never know with Bett. In the same voice she uses to tell you her kitchen is pink, she'll tell you her trailer burned down, or she has some weird lump on her leg that won't go away. Talking with her on the phone I realize that I'm strangling the receiver. That I have stopped breathing.

My fears are not unwarranted. News of Bett's life comes to me in pieces, usually well after the harrowing events. Just last year I found out that she had a miscarriage when she was living in Little Rock that almost killed her, and it wasn't her first miscarriage either, another thing I discovered. And it wasn't til a few months ago that I learned Russell had beaten her—I hope not more than once— which resulted in her leaving him, which was the reason he drove his truck into that tree. And there are other things, things that happened in Lubbock, I wish I'd never heard. And god only knows the stories she hasn't shared.

What is remarkable, what Barbara and I can't understand, is the way Bett reacts to all this mayhem and loss. She never complains about her life, not in that whiny, poor me way the rest of us do. She jokes about it. Bett is the best mimic, the funniest person I know. The time I visited her in Little Rock she described a cop who stopped her for going the wrong way on a one way street, and I was laughing so hard I couldn't hold myself up. Waving her beer and cigarette she did a sensational impersonation of him, even making the veins in her neck stand out to illustrate his aggravation.

"Did he give you a ticket?" I said, wiping my eyes.

"A ticket! Hell they took my *license*. That's why Donny had to take me to the airport to meet you. I don't have a car anymore."

I sat upright on her dingy sofa. "What! They took your license for *that*?"

Bett took a last drag off her cigarette and stubbed it out. "Lorrie, it was like the fourth time I'd gone down that street the wrong way. They'd stopped me for other things too." She lifted her beer and shrugged. "So now I don't drive. That guy Donny?—he's a janitor where I work—he gives me rides when I need them. And I don't miss driving, I really don't." She grinned at me. "I suck at it."

This is what I mean about Bett. News that would cripple most people just slides right off her. Which is probably why she doesn't mind taking care of old people (she's worked in several nursing homes over the years, no doubt lightening these dismal habitats with her notorious humor). I can't imagine anything more difficult, and less lucrative, than caring for the elderly. All those tired souls, bitter, bewildered, waiting to die. Sponge baths. Bedpans. Colostomy bags.

"How do you do it?" I once asked Bett over the phone. "Isn't it horribly depressing?"

A pause. "Yeah, it is. But Lorrie, *somebody's* gotta do it." She has a gift for that too, saying the truest things in the simplest ways.

It's been a long time since Bett had a job in a nursing home, since Little Rock, I think. I wonder if all that misery finally caught up with her; the jobs she takes on now keep her away from people. In Pine Bluff she worked for a dog groomer; in Memphis she had a job in a decal factory, and those five months she lived in Dickson I think she worked the graveyard shift at a donut shop. She doesn't talk about these jobs, doesn't share any riotous anecdotes the way she used to. A lot about Bett has changed in the last couple years and that scares me.

For one thing, she never mentions friends, says she likes being alone. Bett always had friends, clusters of them wherever she went. She could walk into a drugstore and come out five minutes later with a new chum at her side.

And she doesn't write letters anymore. She used to write these long exuberant letters, overflowing with funny asides and heart-stopping truths. Even though I couldn't decipher some of her phrases, couldn't always navigate her turns of thought, I loved those chatty accounts of her life. Now there is just an occasional postcard. A handful of words that don't tell me enough.

I want to call her this very minute—it's maddening she doesn't have a phone. I need to know that her methods aren't failing her, that she has managed one more night of safety.

Murphy is winding around my legs; he smells the chicken I brought him.

"Buk?" he asks, looking up at me.

"Okay. Give me a minute." I take the chicken leg out of the to-go box, pull off the skin, then wash off the lemon-garlic marinade and drop the whole thing in his bowl. Predictably, he seizes the limb, kills it with a shake of his head and drags it out of the dish. It'll take him a while to eat it and there will be splinters and grease on the floor, but he loves pretending that he's ferocious and a bone brings out the beast in him. Right away I hear crunching and then a warning growl that makes me laugh. His eyes are closed, his tail is slowly waving, and I know he is not in this kitchen anymore but on some African plain hunched over a warm impala.

Sipping wine on the sofa I gaze at my fish for several minutes before I notice a zebra danio belly up and bobbing on the surface. This depresses me more than usual, maybe because I've been thinking about Bett and wondering if she's okay. And what makes me feel even worse is flicking the tiny striped body out of the net and into the trash can where it falls between some egg shells and coffee grounds.

I didn't toil hard enough tonight to exhaust myself, so I turn on the television in the bedroom and watch the last half of Bonanza, the episode where Little Joe's girlfriend gets shot and he goes quietly insane. Lorne Green of course comes to his rescue and during a scene where he's studying his son, his face carved with manly concern, I let myself believe in him, in the same way I believed Brian Keith and Buddy Ebsen and all those other television dads who were nothing like my own. Each morning I used to pray to God that when I came down to breakfast Fred MacMurray would be sitting in my father's chair.

Murphy hoists himself up on the bed and, purring deeply, begins to wash himself. I watch a couple minutes of news: Reagan campaigning for a second term, Nancy beside him, a thin smile frozen on her face; more scenes from the tidal wave disaster in Bangladesh; a riot at a soccer match in Brussels—41 people dead. Changing channels I come across a show on how to paint, and then another on monkeys, which I stay with til one of the monkeys is stillborn and the mother, undaunted, tries for days to nurture it, patiently picking off its fleas, even offering the little corpse some of her favorite leaves. How did they get that footage? What sort of person could film such a thing? I turn off the TV, say goodnight to Murphy, then pull down the covers and get into bed.

There's a breeze tonight and through my window comes a primal smell of dirt and wet wood, then the frantic ringing of the windchimes. I lie on my back and think of Bett in her own bed on the other side of the country.

She is wide awake, fingering the buttons on the pink pajamas I sent her last year. The room is damp and the sheets smell musty, like old canvas. Except for a small yellow glow coming from the nightlight, the room is dark and filled with the chirping of frogs and crickets. Behind her head, just outside the window, a horned owl passes. She hears the muffled flap of its wings, the single, chilling shriek.

EIGHT

First thing the next morning I phone Barbara to see if Bett may have tried calling her. Bett tends to do that—no one hears a thing for three months, and then all at once she makes a string of calls. Sure enough Barbara spoke with her, briefly—til the quarters ran out.

"I told her to call me back collect, but you know how she is. She said someone was waiting to use the phone."

"Maybe they were," I say, taking a sip of coffee.

"Maybe. Anyway, nothing's wrong—I guess. She says she likes Burkes Pond, that the people are nice. And you're right about her job—she works at the boat rental, fishing boats. The lake isn't big enough for water skiing."

"What about her cabin?"

"She says it's really a summer cabin but they told her she can stay through the winter if she wants and they'll cut the rent in half."

"Which means it's probably not insulated. Is there a furnace at least?"

"No," Barbara sighs, "just a woodburning stove. And that dog she adopted? It's deaf—wouldn't you know?"

I stare at the coffee table, shake my head.

"How did she sound?"

"Okay, I guess. I don't think she'd been drinking. I asked her what she did when she wasn't working and she said she goes fishing or she takes walks with the dog."

"What else did she say? How big is the town?"

"The population is 42 but Bett says you might as well say 41 because, as she put it, 'Otis Hempel is 94 and not feeling too good.'"

This is just the sort of remark we expect from Bett and it makes us both laugh. Still there's fear, a small dark shape moving through my thoughts.

"Has she made any friends? Did she mention anybody?"

"No….but I didn't ask. I did ask her if she needed anything and of course she said no. Then I asked her if she wanted some books, that I have quite a few I could send her, and she said don't bother, that she hasn't read a book in months. Isn't that strange?"

It is. Bett is never without something to read, and she isn't picky either. She'll go to a garage sale, grab a dozen paperbacks and finish them in as many days.

"Great—I just sent her some books. A Larry McMurtry gift set."

"Oh she'll like those," Barbara says, her voice reassuring. I know just how she looks right now, her face tilted, her deep brown eyes alight with kindness—Barbara is the only person I know whose eyes actually sparkle.

"Guess what?" she says brightly. "She's going to send us a picture. She bought one of those throw-away cameras and a tourist took a picture of her yesterday, with the dog of course. She calls him Spook—he startles easily because of the deafness."

I smile gently and run a slow hand down Murphy's back; his chin, resting on my thigh, is hot and heavy and there's a small spot of drool on my jeans. Barbara and I talk about Bett a little longer, speculating on the town's resources and what the grocery store is like and whether there's a medical clinic. Food, shelter, healthcare—that's all we want for Bett, all we dare hope for.

After that I tell Barbara about Ginger, how she captured my heart the moment I saw her. I tell her about the street she lives on and the clothes she wears and what her father is like, the things he said to me.

"You took her to your house without asking them?"

"I told you—they weren't there."

"Still, Lorrie, you can't do that. You can't just lead a child away from her house. You could have been arrested for kidnapping! And it's not a good lesson for Ginger either."

Barbara's right, she's always right. It was a dumb thing to do.

"If you want to make friends with Ginger, you have to make friends with her parents," she goes on.

"Barbara, if you could see her father. He's"—I shudder—"he's awful."

"What about the mother?"

I lean back against the sofa and look out the window at the frilly tops of the marijuana plants.

"Definitely not Donna Reed. She drove up when I was sitting on the curb with Ginger and all she did was give me a dirty look and run inside."

"Hmmm," Barbara says. "Well you have to win her over—you don't have a choice." She pauses. "I'm not so sure it's a good idea though, getting involved in a situation like that."

I frown into the phone. "Barbara, this kid has nothing, no one—she's counting on me."

"Just be careful—okay? Keep it light?"

I will, I assure her, pointing out the benefits of this arrangement, the simple joy of reading to a child, the harmlessness of it. Barbara, whose nobody's fool, isn't convinced. I can see her, perched at her breakfast bar, legs crossed, one well-shod foot twitching.

There are things I'd like to share with her. My fears about Ginger, the way she looked at her father. But that's where Barbara would roll her eyes and fold her arms and stop listening.

Thinking hard about Ginger, I don't even notice Sasha, who is sitting on her porch with her leg propped on a pillow and a bag of ice on her knee.

"Hi," she says.

I stop short. "What happened to you?"

She got clipped by another cyclist, Sasha tells me; they both went down. She holds up her forearm, shows me the long bloody scrape, then looks gravely at her knee and starts talking about the possibility of a mild patellar dislocation.

Sasha knows her body like a mechanic knows a car. The bones and ligaments, the arterial paths, how her pancreas works, what her heart rate is. She's going in for Xrays today, which will doubtless confirm her own diagnosis; all she really wants from her doctors is a strategy for speedy healing. Sasha sees her doctors as a pit crew, whose main duty is to get her back on the road in the shortest amount of time.

Joel comes out of the house with a big coffee mug in his hand and Tommy pulls up at almost the same instant.

"Hi," he says, waving the mug at me, "and bye." He bends down and kisses Sasha on the top of her head and she reaches out and pulls on the leg of his painter pants.

"Don't forget about my bike."

"I'll be back by 2," he tells her, then bounds down the steps.

"Is it okay? Your bike?"

"It needs some work. Joel's going to bring it in." She leans back on her hands and I notice the glass beside her filled with what looks like antifreeze.

"What's that?" I point.

"Wheat grass and spirulina."

I don't understand this relationship, an artist and an athlete, one intent on pleasure, the other on pain. While Joel is quick to put an arm around Sasha or give her a kiss, rarely does she reach for him (though I've seen her give her bikes a loving pat plenty of times). I suppose it's the sex that keeps them together—god knows she enjoys herself in that arena. Maybe it's another form of training for her, a way to keep her heart, lungs and lymph system functioning at peak levels when she's not peddling up a mountain.

As usual Ginger is sitting on the curb, only this time she doesn't notice me approach. She is bent over her book and trying to ignore the three boys who are sitting on the opposite curb. The one in the middle is throwing gravel at her feet.

"Ugly Four-Eyes," I hear him say, and the others promptly chime in.

"Ugly Four-Eyes, Ugly Four-Eyes!" they shout.

Another fistful of stones skitters across the asphalt but Ginger doesn't budge. I get close enough to cause concern and the boy who was about to throw more gravel at Ginger, wings it under the parked car beside him. Abruptly all three boys stop chanting. The chubby Hispanic child and the little freckled redhead avert their eyes, but the stone-thrower, smirking, regards me steadily. Ginger's head jerks up when I say hello and I see the surprise and relief in her face. The stone-thrower, a boy with a long face and no chin, scoops up more gravel and, feigning nonchalance, pours it from one hand to the other. He looks about 10 years old.

"Stop being cruel," I tell him. My voice is shaking.

He snorts at this and starts tossing the gravel, a piece at a time, against the car's bumper.

"Does it make you feel good to hurt someone else?" I say. The next stone strikes the chrome sharply. Words won't stop this boy.

"I'll talk to your parents if you do it again," I tell him, but it's more a plea than a warning.

I reach out my hand to Ginger and we walk across the dirt yard to the porch.

"Who's that?" I ask as we sit down. "The one in the middle."

She's been crying and her face is mottled and swollen. She edges a dark look at the curb.

"Jason Webber. I *hate* him."

"Does he bother you a lot?"

She nods and her chin starts to pucker and I take her hand between mine.

"Don't let him throw stones at you," I tell her. "If he tries to do that, go inside. And let me know," I add, squeezing her hand. "Let me know if he's mean to you again."

I notice the television then. A burst of music, canned laughter, the voice of a game show host.

"Are your folks home?"

"My mother is."

I let go of Ginger's hand and glance at the window behind us. Here's your chance, I hear Barbara say. I imagine knocking on the door and my stomach crimps. What will I say? How can I explain myself?

And then I know.

"I want to say hi to your mom," I tell Ginger, getting to my feet. She gives me a puzzled look and stays where she is.

Quickly, before I lose my nerve, I knock on the door. It doesn't open right away and I start to feel lightheaded because my heart is beating so fast. I'm just about to try again when the door is yanked open and there is Ginger's mother, tall and annoyed, behind the screen.

For a second or two I can't speak. She shifts her weight and frowns. "Yeah?"

"Hi!" I say, the word coming out in one big breath. "I'm Lorrie? Lorrie Rivers?" She waits, daring me to say something that will keep her standing there.

"Anyway, I've been talking to Ginger? And she told me you sold cosmetics."

In an instant her whole body changes. She straightens up and her eyes widen and her arm, which was ready to slam the door, drops to her side.

"I was wondering if I could maybe look at some of your products."

The next thing I know she's rushing me into the kitchen and hauling down a sample case from atop the refrigerator. Ginger wanders in behind us and her mother tells her that we're busy and not to bother us. I pull out one of the diningroom chairs and watch Ginger walk down the hallway, running her fingertips along the wall. She reaches a doorway and turns around and grins and I see how thrilled she is that I'm here. I give her a wink, which she returns with much embellishment, tugging her head to one side.

From the layer of dust on the wooden box I can see why Ginger's mother is so keen about the prospect of a sale. I sit there a moment stealing glimpses of the house as she ransacks the drawers and cupboards looking for her catalog. The place is cluttered but not quite as grim as I pictured it. There's pinto-colored shag carpeting in the livingroom and a set of orange vinyl furniture and a coffee table covered with tools and automotive parts. The linoleum in the kitchen is peeling around the edges, and the cabinets, under thick coats of yellow paint, are grimy at the handles. In the middle of the table is an ashtray fashioned like a small tire, its metal rim loaded with butts. A Basset hound in a party hat stares at me from the wall calendar and I notice that someone's been crossing off the days with an X. One more square and they will have survived the month of May.

Having unearthed the catalog, Ginger's mother lights up a Kool and sits down. Parking her cigarette on the ashtray's sidewall, she opens the sample case and reveals dozens of tiny lipsticks and tubes of cream and miniature palettes of eye shadow. Dress-up, I think. Halloween. Looking up from the collection I catch her studying me and immediately she lowers her eyes. She is wearing a purple tube top and I see a flush come up her neck. Her arms are long and freckled, with a few blemishes near the shoulders. Her lips are thin, her nose is sharp and the skin around her eyes is dark and slack. She must have been laying down when I knocked: there's a crease on her left cheek and her curly red hair is mashed on that side. Given Ginger's age, I assume this woman is in her late twenties, but she looks at least a decade older.

"Ginger didn't mention your name," I say.

"Shirley," she says. She has one of those raspy cigarette voices.

"I met your—" I pause. "Husband" just doesn't seem like the right word for the person I met in the driveway.

"Bill," she says, picking up her cigarette and taking a drag. "Our last name's Hebert." She blows a lungful of smoke over the table, then swipes at it. "Sorry."

"So," she says, flipping her thumb at the catalog. "This first page tells you about our make-up and how good it is for your skin. You want to hear it?"

"Sure."

Opening the catalog to the first page, she starts reading to me about hypoallergenics and skin types, halting every few words to figure out where the sentence is going. Seeing her forehead wrinkling with effort, her chipped fingernail tracing the words, I am overcome with sadness and I have to look away.

I order about $75 worth of merchandise, some of which I'm even going to use (the dreary stuff, sunscreen and moisturizer); the rest I'll give to Rita. With painstaking slowness Shirley writes each item number on a form, then rechecks her entries, murmuring each one.

"You're supposed to sign your name here," she says, pointing to a line and pushing the paper towards me. Suddenly, as if remembering a piece of advice, she smiles and I see that her front tooth is chipped. I am struck by the change in her, the hope I have fostered with this sham of a sale. Uncomely, luckless, eager in spite of herself, she is like most everyone else. I sign the order and tell her that it was nice of her to see me without an appointment.

She tucks the form into the catalog and lights up another cigarette. "Usually I go to people's houses. They don't come here."

"Well thank you for letting me come in and do this."

I look around the room, searching for something to compliment her on. My eyes move from the grease-lacquered stovetop, where the gold-tone finish has been scrubbed off in places, to a scorched piece of toast on the counter, to a stained plastic pitcher, and finally to the sprig of yellow flowers stuck in a juice glass on the window ledge.

"Those are pretty," I point.

Shirley looks at the window. "Yeah. Yellow's my favorite color."

"It's Ginger's favorite color too," I say, eager for this chance to talk about her.

"I know that," she says curtly. I feel admonished. It hadn't occurred to me that she might be jealous.

"You must be proud of Ginger," I offer. "She's so smart, such a fast reader."

Shirley rolls her eyes and taps her ash into the tire. "That's all she ever wants to do." She pauses, eyes me curiously. "She showed me those books you brought over—those are nice books. Expensive."

I wave my hand dismissively. "They mean a lot more to her than they do to me. She can keep them."

She stubs out her cigarette and shrugs.

I lean forward. "Shirley?"

Startled, she looks up from the ashtray.

"Do you mind me coming over here and reading to Ginger? Is it okay with you?"

A silence blooms. I hold my breath, keep my eyes wide and innocent. Shirley clears her throat, looks over at the window.

"Well, Bill don't like it, but I don't care." She turns to me, arches a plucked eyebrow. "Keeps her out of *my* hair." She grins at me, I grin back, and there's my hole in the fence.

She offers up everything after that, a cup of Sanka, a piece of toast, even tells me a little about her family in Lodi (she's one of nine children). I tell her I'm from Vermont, which she thinks is very exotic, and that I'm a cook, which makes her grimace.

After the Sanka, she takes me into her room and shows me a charcoal drawing of a horse in a meadow with a barn in the background. It's not bad.

"I did that," she beams. "I learned through the mail."

"You should frame it," I tell her, noting the thumbtacks and split edges. "To protect it."

"Yeah," she nods. "I really should."

I glance around the room, taking in the cheap metal bedframe, the heap of clothes in the corner, the scarred blonde dresser strewn with those little china animals you buy at the drugstore. I feel like I'm looking for clues, though I'm not sure to what.

Ginger slides into the doorway and we turn to look at her. She holds up Charlotte's Web with both hands.

"Can she read to me now? We're almost at the end."

Shirley puts her hands on her hips and cocks her head at Ginger. "Yes she can read to you now," she says, mimicking Ginger's voice. She turns to me, hesitates.

"You can read in the house if you want." She lifts a shoulder, indicating her indifference.

"Oh!" Ginger says, all excited. "Can we read in my room?"

Shirley says she guesses so and we cross the hall into Ginger's room, a dim rectangle with coffee-colored walls and one window too high for her to see out of. The room is so narrow that the bed has to be pushed against the wall. In the opposite corner is a card table and a folding chair. The only other piece of furniture is a small green dresser. Ginger shows me her coloring books, each picture neatly filled in, then hands me a piece of yellow construction paper with a sparkly rainbow arching across it. "I love rainbows," she breathes, tracing a line of blue sparkles with her finger. Taped to the walls are pictures scissored from magazines, animals mostly: a bear with two cubs, a trio of dolphins, a kitten playing with a ball of yarn, a sleeping lion. She asks me if I can bring her a picture of a sea turtle and I tell her I most certainly can.

After this tour Ginger climbs onto the bed and I pull out the chair and start reading about Charlotte's last days on earth and the three baby spiders who decide to stay with Wilbur, and at some point Shirley slips into the room and settles next to Ginger, and it's hard to say which one looks more devastated when I come to the end of the story.

NINE

Somewhere in this world are home movies of me and my sisters taken on a beach in Alabama when we were very young. No sound, just scene after scene of Barbara, Bett and me building sandcastles, catching hermit crabs, running full speed into the foamy, sluggish waves or bobbing around in my father's giant yellow military raft. Filmed over three summers these movies contain our lost selves, and if I could view them again, if I could examine each look and gesture, I might discover who we were and just how far we've drifted.

But that's not likely to happen. My mother, who molts her past with each divorce, left the reels of film, along with the screen and projector, in the basement of our house in Vermont and god knows what became of them after she sold the place. Most likely they're rusting away in some municipal dump.

She's not long on sentiment, my mother. As a birthday present one year I made her a photo album, a painstaking project I spent months compiling, arranging sackfuls of pictures into a tidy family chronology. She left that gift with her second husband, along with my grandmother's china, a Boston rocker my grandfather had made, and the silhouettes my father painted, twenty years before, of Barbara, Bett and me. The rest of our remnants disappeared with husband number three, who I'm sure lost no time discarding them. Now my mother is surrounded with factory furnishings she purchased in one afternoon at a strip mall and aside from our high school graduation pictures, you'd be hard pressed to find any sign of us in her Fort Myers double wide.

I can understand my mother's desire to put some distance between herself and the lousy men she chose, but I wish she hadn't sheared away from us in the process. We have talked, Barbara, Bett and I, about my mother's defection, how remote she's become in recent years. When Barbara and I visited her in Florida, not long after she moved there, she seemed pleased, even grateful, that we came, but she was nervous the whole time and I could feel her relief when we left. Waiting at the airport for our flights Barbara and I discussed this, Barbara arguing that our mother had never been "the June Cleaver type." But it was Bett who surmised the truth, or what I've come to believe is the truth.

We were sitting on swings in a tiny park near her trailer in Little Rock. It was a humid evening and the sun was sliding behind the elm trees and sky above was hot pink. Bett was looking at her arm, watching a mosquito swell with blood, and I asked her how often she got a phone call from our mother.

"Never. And whenever I call her she wants to hang up after five minutes. Says someone's at the door, or that she needs to take a roast out of the oven—like she cooks."

I tapped the ground with my feet, sending up small clouds of dirt. "She doesn't call me either," I said. "Don't you think that's weird?"

Bett, apparently satisfied with the mosquito's girth, smashed it with her palm, then wiped her blood-smeared arm on her jeans. She turned to me, and with the sun so low I could see her eyes through her glasses, her small weak eyes; crossed at birth, they required two surgeries.

"Lorrie, don't you see? She on the lam. From *us*."

I looked at her blankly.

"She's scared to death that one of us is going to ask her why she didn't protect us. Why she didn't stop him."

That's what we call our father: Him. We can't bring ourselves to use the word Dad.

TEN

"I don't think so, Rita."

"You'd like her," Rita insists, "you two have a lot in common."

"That's what you said about Jules."

Jules is Rita's dentist. I went out with her, once, mainly to placate Rita, who has long been distressed by my single status and who has apparently made it her mission to find me a mate. This date was the most hideous I've ever experienced, three hours of listening to a woman describe her last days with a partner who died of breast cancer. Although this death had occurred some eight months previous, Jules's grief engulfed the bar we were sitting in and even the people who could not hear her were edging uncomfortable glances our way. But even if she'd been a fun and witty conversationalist that night (and she did try at one point to rally), I never would have gone out with her a second time. She was bad business, that woman, a sea of need; instinctively I kept edging my chair back. Plus, I didn't find her physically appealing. Someone else might have admired her slender body, her exotic face, but for me she was too small and too thin, and her eyes bugged out, just a little but just enough; and I really didn't like her lips. Sexual attraction is the one arena where bias is allowed, and this is my rule about lips: whomever I sleep with has to have them.

Rita groans. Jules is a running joke between us.

"Okay, would you give me a break about Jules? Anyway, Sharon is nothing like Jules."

"This doesn't reflect well on me, but what does she look like?"

"She's cute. Athletic-looking. Short blonde hair—*great* hair."

"So she's a customer?"

"Oh yeah. She saw my ad in the Lavender Pages."

"What does she do?"

"She works at a plant nursery in Oakland. She moved here a few months ago from the South bay. She lives in north Berkeley, on Hearst, I think."

"How old is she?"

"I don't know—35-ish? Maybe older. Don't worry—she's been around the block." This is by way of encouragement; Rita knows I'm not generally attracted to younger women.

"You're asking a lot of questions for someone who isn't interested," Rita says. "Listen, she's nice and she works with plants—you can get a discount—and when she comes in she brings her own reading material, won't touch that mass market crap I have to buy."

I take a deep breath and look at Murphy, who is laying next to me on the back steps, soaking in a pool of sun.

"Okay," I say. "But not an evening thing."

"Breakfast!" Rita pounces. "You can meet at the Brick Hut."

I frown, reconsidering. "God I hate this staged stuff, Rita."

"Don't take it so seriously. What are we talking here—toast and coffee, an hour out of your life." She pauses. "You want her phone number instead? I could get it."

I imagine calling her, trying to introduce myself.

"No. I'll just meet her at the Brick Hut."

"She has Mondays and Tuesdays off."

I change position and let the sun seep into my back. "Next Tuesday, I guess. See if that's okay with her."

"You're really going to like her," Rita says.

I roll my eyes at Murphy, who yawns and stretches his legs, then switch the phone to my other ear.

"I don't know why you insist on fixing me up. I'm fine, you know. My life is full. I work, I garden, I go to movies. And Ginger. I read to her a couple times a week."

"That little girl?" says Rita. "You're still going over there? What about the mother?"

"It's the father I'm worried about. I've managed to make friends, well sort of, with Ginger's mother. She's okay. Kind of pathetic. Comes from a big litter in Lodi." Rita laughs.

"I feel sorry for her," I go on. "I mean I hate the way she neglects Ginger, but I don't think she does it out of meanness. I just think she's not smart enough to know how important parenting is. She's not the type who beats the odds; she did what everyone expected—got into the wrong car with the wrong guy and kept going. Probably she got pregnant."

"How did you make friends with her?"

"Ginger told me she sold make-up—you know, door to door? So I bought some from her. By the way, next week you're getting an armload of mascara and eye liner."

"Neat," Rita says. "So what about the father? What's he like?"

My stomach tightens as his image comes back to me. That pinched face. Those close-set, squinty eyes. "Ignorant," I say. "Ignorant and aggressive."

"The worst combination," Rita murmurs. "So you've spoken with him?"

"Just once. He was working on his truck. He was awful, asked me didn't I have anything better to do than hang around Ginger. I saw him again yesterday and he ignored me."

"Ignore him back. The mother's on your side, right?"

I reach out and stroke Murphy's hot gold fur. "Yes, but I think he might resent me even more because of it. He's definitely not thrilled about my visits and I'm afraid he might pull that, you know, 'I'm the boss' shit and not let me come over anymore."

"And you're probably right," she says, and then she reminds me that like it or not, he is the father and I am nobody and my association with Ginger is bound to cause trouble and it sounds like it already has. Like Barbara, she doesn't want to see me get hurt, and I appreciate that, but she may as well be cautioning me in Arabic for all I care. I can't expect her to understand what Ginger means to me; I am still trying to understand it myself.

We talk a little longer and then I hear Sheree say something to Rita and I know it's time to get off the phone. Sheree doesn't quite trust my familiarity with Rita, much as I try to demonstrate my harmlessness when I'm around the two of them. Rita says that Sheree has some "abandonment issues" that they're working on. I have heard this sort of thing so many times that it makes me wonder if there are any lesbian couples in this town who love each other just for fun.

"Hey!" I say just as we're about to hang up. "How will Sharon and I recognize each other? Do want me to wear a hat? A red scarf? Or maybe I should hold up a sign like they do at the airport."

"I've already got that figured out. I'll tell Sharon to look for a gorgeous woman with silver hair." Rita can be awfully charming.

"Thanks. What should I be looking for?"

"A butch blonde with a rash."

I let out a laugh that makes Murphy jump, and then say, "You *were* kidding?"

After we hang up I lean back on my hands and survey the backyard, admiring the pretty ribbons of corn, the green bursts of leaf lettuce, the obedient peas climbing up their trellis, the exuberant marijuana plants, which, wide as they are tall, are now shading the tomatoes. Joel has an instinct for growing pot, knowing precisely what to do and when, employing his own theories and potions. Having dosed them for weeks with a secret fishy liquid, he is now slipping them something that boosts the growth of flowers and those tiny white hairs are popping up everywhere. The tomatoes, in comparison, won't be bearing much fruit, but this is an acceptable loss.

I have the place to myself today. Joel and Tommy are surfing at Stinson Beach. As often as they can in the summer months they throw their boards in Tommy's box van and spend the day zipped up in wet suits waiting for the right wave. Mostly that's what they do, wait. Walk along any Marin county beach and you'll see a string of young men sitting on surfboards in that frigid kelp-strewn water. Once in a while a wave comes along that sparks hope and some of these men leap up and try to ride it. One or two fall off, others manage to stay on for a few thrilling seconds before the wave, nearly always a disappointment, collapses beneath them. Then they all paddle back out and do it again, and again, and again, as if they'll never learn. Joel laughs when I ask him what makes it fun, but he's never really explained.

Sasha, meanwhile, is back up on Grizzly Peak preparing her knee for another race, this one in Big Sur. Her injury has healed more rapidly than the doctors predicted and given the exacting diet and regimen she adheres to I'm not surprised.

Sasha doesn't have a job, hasn't worked a day in the two years I've been here: how does she pay her bills? She doesn't win enough races to make up for the time she spends training and it's unlikely that Joel could support them both on the money he makes painting murals. She must be living off a trust or inheritance; there is something about her stance, her cool disregard, that suggests privilege—I know that her folks live in one of those enormous houses on the other side of Telegraph. But Sasha is no spoiled profligate. Beyond what it takes to keep her peddling, she spends nothing, and that's what I envy: not her money but her lack of interest in it.

I'm tempted to stretch out on the chaise longue and read and daydream til I have to go to work. But it's a perfect morning for a walk and I keep thinking about the promise I made to Barbara: next time we talk she'll surely want to know if I've applied at the university yet. I pet Murphy once more, then go inside and look in my closet for an outfit more appropriate than the tank top and shorts I'm wearing.

I don't want to dodge the sidewalk vendors, nor do I want to breathe in the mingled funk of bagels and falafels, car exhaust and street people, so I bypass Telegraph and take a quieter route to the university, admiring along the way the sleepy old houses in my neighborhood with their canted porches and mossy shingles. I brush past a hedge of honeysuckle and the scent stays on my arm. Several times the smell of bacon wafts my way. I hear the crying of a newborn, the shriek of someone's parrot, piano music. An older couple practice Tai Chi under the ferny branches of a redwood. A woman with a blue-eyed hound walks by and the dog gives my leg a quick sniff.

With its august buildings and rolling green expanses, the UC Berkeley campus might have been plucked from antiquity and placed here by some powerful god. There is even a slight blurring around the edges of things as if this whole dreamy vista might float away at any moment. I half-expect to see toga-clad orators gathered on the grassy knolls, brawny naked athletes throwing a discus. Instead there are Asians in brightly colored windbreakers, bejeweled black men from the Ivory Coast, dark-eyed Arabs, long-legged Swedes. No one, it appears, takes this school lightly and I am struck by the measured behavior of the students, the high seriousness in which they're engaged. The college I attended was small and homogeneous, the dormitories within staggering distance of the classrooms. Six-packs hung from the windows, the Grateful Dead was always playing and most everyone I knew started the day with a bong hit. No Greek god would have touched the place.

I find the human resource building without much trouble and am thrown into the modern world as soon as I cross the threshold. Everyone is sitting in front of a computer or typewriter and the room is humming with electricity and purpose. Unable to catch anyone's eye, I ease over to the job board and look for something, anything, I might be able to do. What interests me most are the listings in the biology department and my heart leaps when I see an ad at a bottom of the board for "Frog Embryo Maintenance." Briefly I imagine myself monitoring dozens of jelly jars filled with tadpoles, but it seems there might be more to it as even this job, which pays only a little more than I make now, requires "a degree in biology or biochemistry and extensive training in molecular techniques." There are of course plenty of clerical jobs, for which I'm equally unqualified, and some openings in campus security that require a background in law enforcement and a valid driver's license. I refuse to check the listings under "Dining Services."

One of the women in the office looks at me, draws conclusions and turns back to her computer. Feeling as though my uselessness is visible I cross the room and let myself out.

There's still time before work to sit on the chaise longue and go through my back issues of National Wildlife. What I'm looking for are pictures of sea turtles for Ginger and right away I find an article on Hawaiian reefs that contains two good photos. One is a belly shot—the pale segmented underside of a green sea turtle moving through blue water; the other, which Ginger will love, is a picture of a woman snorkeling alongside a large spotted turtle. They look like friends.

I carefully tear these pages out, then pick up another issue and immediately become engrossed in an article on whales. Somehow they've managed to take a close-up of a humpback's "face," and the effect is disturbing. Now, for the price of a magazine, millions of people can gape at the eye of a whale, and this is no flat fish eye, this one is eerily human, shaped elliptically, with a pupil and an iris and white crescents on either side. There is something terrible about it, a vulnerability that shames me. Impossible that in the cold rubbery case of a sea beast one should find this mortal window. It must contain every secret there is.

This is probably the only picture among the hundreds available here that wouldn't be suitable for Ginger's wall and I spend several happy minutes making my selections: a porpoise swimming with her calf, a penguin jumping off a rock, a sea otter munching on abalone, a sleeping polar bear, four young Arctic foxes, a pair of fawns, an orange cloud of butterflies. Studying this last photo reminds me of the cottony cocoons I used to find on the backs of leaves. How thrilling it was to imagine—a butterfly from a caterpillar! Sometimes it comes back to me, just for an instant, the wonder and terror. The place where children live.

ELEVEN

What a stupid thing to do—pour out the soup while it was still tucked inside the double boiler. That scalding water had nowhere to go but down my arm. Just before the pain there was a sharp coldness that took my breath and voice away, as if with one deft yank someone had ripped off my skin. I let go the soup and looked down, and there on the inside of my forearm was a bubbly blister the size of my fist.

I couldn't speak for a couple minutes, not that I really needed to. Zee, who heard the soup tureen crash into the sink, gave me a towel full of ice, then herded me to her car and drove me to Alta Bates—luckily this happened at the end of our shift. In the ER they gave me a blue plastic tub filled with ice water in which I submerged my arm til it went numb, then pulled it out, then plunged it back in. Stinging cold or searing pain—I had my choice. It was monotonous but it did keep me occupied for the 55 minutes I sat there.

The doctor, a red-haired man with a big bland face, gave me a tetanus shot and a pain pill, then wrapped gauze around my arm and, without changing expression, told me some of the worst jokes I've ever heard. When I was all bandaged up and hurrying to the door (hospitals terrify me), he said, pleasantly, "Come back tomorrow—we have to take off the dead skin. You'll heal faster that way."

It's after midnight when I pull open the glass doors and step out into the fog-dampened June night. I told Zee not to wait for me, that I'd call for a taxi. That was a lie. Maybe it's their furtive manner, or the desperate way they drive, or their mugshots leering from the dashboard, but cab drivers make me nervous and I'm not about to convenience one of them by getting into his car, all alone, in the middle of the night.

As always, I feel perfectly safe walking through this town. I am no different, at this hour, from the other scattered souls on the street and we nod at one other and say hello. For private, maybe painful, reasons we are not in our beds: we need to be acknowledged. Such courtesies may be fruitless in the day time, but now they strike deep, now they are comfort.

I am wounded. That's all I know, all I am. I cradle my arm, walk cautiously. It's a form of hypochondria. Two months ago I lost a large filling; it fell into the sink while I was brushing my teeth. Panicking, I wrapped it in Kleenex as if it were a fingertip and ran to the phone. I had to wait until the next day to be restored, and all that night I kept running my tongue over the hole in my tooth, alarming myself anew.

Some dogs, I've heard, can sense the onset of an epileptic seizure; some can detect the growth of cancer cells. I think Murphy might be equally intuitive. When I settle down on the sofa he leaps up beside me, sniffs my bandage, then squints in surprise. "I burned myself," I tell him and he looks at me with grave concern.

Halfway through my glass of wine, a stupor comes over me and I can hardly keep my eyes open. The trauma of my injury, I suppose, or maybe the effects of that pain pill? Come to think of it, I probably shouldn't be drinking. I get to my feet and make it to the bathroom without mishap and slowly wash my face and right forearm—the doctor used lots of gauze and my burned arm is concealed almost to the wrist. Ginger will be very impressed.

Anticipating my next move, Murphy is already on the bed. I know he's still worried about me because he isn't laying down.

"Murph," I whisper. Bending forward, I place my forehead lightly against his and in a few seconds he is purring and his fat gold paws start lifting off the covers. "Lay down, Murphy," I say, patting the bed, and he does.

I have to shift around several times to find a position that won't put pressure on my burn. It still hurts, but the pain is manageable now, reminding of jellyfish and bee stings. I lie on my back and think about my mother, who I'm sure is sitting in her kitchen drinking Taster's Choice and working on a crossword puzzle; haunted, restless, she's almost always up before dawn, a mania she's passed on to me. Barbara, who is also three hours away, is dreaming alongside her husband. In 45 minutes her alarm will beep and she'll reach across her reading glasses, novel and cortisone cream to turn it off.

Bett, I hope, is sleeping peacefully. When I spent those five days with her in Little Rock, we shared a bed and every night I heard her moaning in her sleep— she's always done that; it used to annoy me when we were kids.

During that visit she slept with the hall light on. I asked her why and she said that she hadn't bought a new bulb for her nightlight yet. This made me smile. "You're afraid of the dark?"

"No, I just don't like it."

"Why?"

She took off her glasses, put them on the nightstand and rolled onto her side. Her back was facing me.

"Because that's when he came into our room."

My mind repeats those words til I am sufficiently numb to them, and then, as if in solace, I am given a memory of something nice, a game Bett and I used to play when we were children.

We called it "Boat." I would be in my bed, Bett in hers, and we would share fantasies about a boat that would take us far far away, a boat filled with everything we could ever want. I would opt for a swimming pool, Bett would add a movie theater; I would vote for a hundred bags of popcorn, Bett would insist on a room filled with chocolate.

I see it now, a white yacht in a blue lagoon. Bett is on board and leaning over the railing. The breeze is lifting her fine blonde hair. She is grinning, motioning to me. "C'mon," she is calling, "C'mon!"

"What happened to your arm?" Ginger says when I walk up. She steps off the porch, eyes my bandage, her mouth pursed in awe.

"It's a burn," I tell her. "A bad one. I spilled boiling water down my arm."

"Really?" she breathes. "Can I see it?"

I shake my head. "I'm not supposed to take off the bandage, because of germs."

"Oh." She frowns, then her eyes widen. "What if we just *peek* at it. You could pull off the bandage just a little bit and then you could put it back." She nods at me encouragingly.

"Okay." I put down my backpack and Ginger edges closer. With slow drama I peel up a corner of the bandage. Ginger clasps her hands under her chin and cringes in preparation.

"See it?" I say, extending my arm. She tilts her head, peers under the gauze.

"Ewwwwww!" she cries, mugging horror. "Does it hurt?"

"It hurt real bad yesterday, but now it only hurts a little." I widen my eyes, drop my voice to a whisper. "But guess what?"

She takes a step closer. "What?"

"Today the doctor has to"—I wince—"cut off the dead skin."

Ginger covers her mouth with her hands. "Ewwwwww." Abruptly her expression turns solemn. "Will it hurt?"

"I don't know."

She crosses her arms, nods in certainty. "It'll hurt," she says.

A small red ball smacks against the aluminum screen door, barely missing Ginger and me. It ricochets back, bounces down the steps and drops into the dead shrubbery beside the porch. I turn and look at the four boys across the street, recognizing the chubby Hispanic child and then Jason Webber, who, baseball bat in hand, is slouching in his driveway. I stand there a moment, eyeing him, wondering if this was intentional.

"Hey!" he calls. "Throw it back."

"Don't give it to him," Ginger says.

"Has he done that before, hit your house?"

"No," she says. "But I know he did it on purpose. He likes to scare me."

I walk down the steps, pull the ball out of the bushes and toss it into the street; the Hispanic boy jogs out to get it.

"He'll just do it again," Ginger says.

"Maybe not," I tell her. "Let's wait and see. He hasn't thrown any more gravel at you, has he?" She shakes her head, scowls.

Today she is wearing chocolate brown pants and a yellow shirt that's too small for her. As usual she is barefoot.

"You're not wearing a dress."

She frowns. "I know. My mom has to do a wash."

"Well I think you look very nice." I stick out my foot and show her my red sneakers. "Do you like my new shoes?" I ask, hiking up my jeans. "See? They're called high-tops." Ginger studies them.

"They come in blue and green and yellow too."

She raises her eyebrows, nods politely.

"Do you have any sneakers?"

She shakes her head. "I only have hard shoes."

What I really want to do is take her shopping, a whole day of it. We could go out to eat somewhere, her choice. Or I could make her something: a tower of tiny sandwiches, watermelon balls, brownies in the shape of stars.

"Where's your mom?" I ask. The Galaxie isn't in the driveway (nor is the truck her father drives, thank god).

"She had to go to the store. She says not to start reading without her."

"Okay," I smile. This is a habit we're getting into. I read to Ginger in the livingroom while Shirley, seated at the kitchen table in front of her new sketchbook, listens. She's been trying to draw a lion, using Ginger's sleeping lion photo as a guide, but the work isn't going well and she spends more time erasing than she does sketching. She blames the lighting, among other things.

"Where's your father?"

Ginger shrugs. "*I* don't know."

"He's gone a lot, isn't he?"

She sighs. "He has to pick up things. He has to drive to lots of places."

Drugs. Or black market peddling.

Ginger twirls her hair; it's all snarled on that side, and once again it doesn't look very clean.

The boys start to shout and I see they've whacked the ball into the gutters of the house behind them. Jason swears, throws down the bat. Out of the corner of my eye I see the Rottweiller get to his feet; immediately I turn back to Ginger: I can't look at that dog anymore.

"We can go inside," she says. "We can watch TV."

This doesn't seem like a good idea, especially if Ginger's father decides to show up.

"Let's just wait out here. She won't be long."

Ginger heaves a sigh, lifts her shoulders. "Okay but what are we going to *do*?"

"Tell me what your favorite foods are."

In a show of concentration she tilts her head and frowns. Her lips move, the upper working over the lower—Bett!

"Cheese," she says. "And animal crackers. And hot dogs. And pudding."

"What about popcorn?"

She nods vigorously.

"Jello?"

She nods again and grins. "Keep asking me," she says, hugging her knees.

Just then Shirley pulls into the drive. She waves when she sees me and I consider how far I've come in three weeks. I watch her shove open the door and swing her long chalk-colored legs out of the car. Today she's wearing red short shorts and a blue sleeveless top. Her hair is long and messy. She looks excited about something. Me?

"I've got lunch," she says, holding up a grocery bag. She drops her cigarette and scuffs it into the dirt. "Give me ten minutes."

"Jason hit a ball at our door," Ginger says.

Shirley looks across the street, then back at us.

"Hey." She points at my arm. "What did you do to your arm?"

"She *burned* it," Ginger says. "It's really bad."

"I was pouring out soup," I explain, "and the water underneath it scalded me. Really dumb."

"Can she see it?" Ginger asks me.

"*I* don't want to see it!" Shirley says, brushing past us to the door. "You know I hate that stuff." She pulls open the door and goes inside. "Are you coming in or what?" she calls through the screen, and we follow her into the house.

"Don't look at the mess," she says. "I haven't had time to clean."

Glancing into the kitchen I can see why. The tire ashtray is full of butts and there are pink erasure bits all over the table. Apparently Shirley has abandoned the sleeping lion and chosen one of the photographs I gave Ginger, the penguin jumping into the ocean. So far she has drawn the big gray rock and, with a whimsy that moves me, a starfish that isn't in the photo.

The place does look worse than usual: dishes piled in the sink and on the countertops, trashcan overflowing. Shirley shoves some glasses aside and starts unpacking her sack of groceries.

"You can't watch me," she says. "You'll make me nervous."

I put my hands up in a gesture of apology and move into the livingroom where Ginger, anxious to hear more of Black Beauty, is already sitting.

"Don't start reading yet," Shirley says, "I have to concentrate on this." She pauses, looks up. "It's only 11:00. I hope you're hungry."

"*I* am!" Ginger says.

Shirley snorts. "You're always hungry." She nods toward the trashcan. "Why don't you dump the garbage while you're waiting?"

Reluctantly Ginger pushes herself off the couch and with slow tiny steps makes her way to the kitchen.

"It's only going to take longer that way," says Shirley, who is rummaging through the fridge.

Ginger pauses for just a second, then continues her laborious journey, and watching her I can't help but smile. She may not have Bett's nerve but she sure shares her stubbornness.

I am touched by the lunch Shirley makes us: bologna and cheese sandwiches on hamburger buns, individual bowls of potato chips and fruit cocktail spooned into juice glasses. She has even bought curly parsley to garnish our plates and long straws for the rootbeer.

"*Hamburger* buns?" Ginger says in bewildered disbelief. She picks up the sprig of parsley and waves it about. "What's this?"

"It's parsley," Shirley says. "You don't eat it. It's for show."

With disdain Ginger drops it back on her plate.

"How come you put the potato chips in *bowls*?"

"Hush up and eat your lunch," Shirley says. "Christ. Can't I do something different once in a while?"

"It all looks great," I assure her. "I like your idea of putting the sandwiches on these sesame buns."

Shirley blushes fiercely and hooks a straggly lock of hair behind her ear.

"Well I know it's not as fancy as what you're used to, being a chef."

Ginger begins eating potato chips, one after another, until Shirley pulls the bowl away and tells her to eat her sandwich.

"It's great," I say to Ginger, taking a bite from mine. "Nothing hits the spot like bologna."

Ginger eyes me a moment, then picks up her sandwich. "I know," she nods, her glasses flashing under the fluorescent light.

"You see I started a new drawing," Shirley says, pointing at the sketchpad, which has been pushed, along with most of the erasure leavings, to the edge of the table.

I nod enthusiastically and tell her the starfish is a nice touch. She beams at this and confides that the lion just didn't have enough life in it and she likes drawing action pictures better. We start talking then about adult education classes and I tell her how cheap they are and that she could probably take a drawing course—if she wanted to—and only have to pay for supplies. If she took a morning class, I add, ingeniously, I could look after Ginger while she's gone. Ginger moves her gaze from one of us to the other as we talk, meanwhile blowing bubbles in her rootbeer and picking at the edge of her sandwich bun, creating a fringe all the way around. Shirley, noticing the pile of crumbs on her plate, interrupts me to frown at her daughter.

"Now why did you do that? That looks awful."

Ginger's eyes widen in a pretense of fear; she hunches down, grins an apology. I can hear her feet hitting the rung of the chair.

"You'd better stop playing with that thing and eat it," Shirley says, and Ginger, quickly nodding, brings the sandwich to her mouth and takes a monstrous bite.

"And don't be cute," her mother warns.

After lunch Shirley works on her penguin drawing while I read several pages of Black Beauty. Ginger is particularly taken with this story, maybe because there's a mare with her name in it. She is going to have a farm, she has told me, "where the horses can be happy and eat apples and don't get hurt." Now and then I glance up from the page just to see her face and how it changes as I read; she is living every word.

"Shit," Shirley mutters. I hear her pencil hit the table, the click of her lighter.

She has shifted position and is now facing us, her legs crossed, her arm resting on the back of the chair. I smile sympathetically.

"You want me to look into those classes for you?"

She blows a hard stream of smoke out the corner of her mouth. "I guess," she sighs. "I know I can draw better than this."

"Absolutely," I say. "All you need are a few tips and a little more practice."

"Now can we read?" Ginger pleads.

I shake my head regretfully. "I have to leave now. I wish I had more time but I have to stop at the hospital before I go to work." I hold up my bandaged arm. "Because of this."

Ginger folds her arms across her chest and pouts, and just then I hear the truck pull up. Immediately Shirley stubs out her cigarette ("Bill hates it when I smoke," she told me). Ginger turns and looks at the door and I can see her anxiety emerge. She uncrosses her arms, brings them close to her sides, hides her hands in the sofa cushions. The screen swings open and her father comes into the house. He's wearing jeans and a T-shirt and I notice again how skinny he is, how narrow his face. His nose is long, the skin pinched and white at the bridge, and his cheeks are sunk into the bones around them. He flicks an oily lock of hair off his forehead and his small eyes dart around the room. This is the second time he's found me here and clearly he doesn't like the arrangement. I greet him with a false and futile smile and he jerks his head by way of reply.

"Place is a mess," he says, striding past Shirley.

"I know," she says. "I'm going to clean this afternoon."

He opens a kitchen drawer, shuffles through it, yanks opens another.

"Where's the Phillips head I keep in here?" he says.

Shirley frowns. "What's a Phillips head?"

"What do you think it is?" he says. "It's a goddamn screwdriver. You know what a screwdriver is?"

I turn to Ginger then, who is not looking at her father but at the coffee table in front of her. I know what she's doing, the same thing she did when Jason Webber was throwing stones at her. She's pretending he isn't there. I did it too.

I get to my feet and thank Shirley for lunch and then I look at Ginger and say, "Can you walk me to the curb?"

"Yes," she says, jumping up.

As soon as the screen door shuts behind us I feel like I can breathe, like I've broken through the surface of a black ocean and suddenly there is sky. Even here. I look at the dead ficus in the clay pot, the cigarette butts in the other, and I get an idea.

"Do you want to grow your very own garden?" I ask Ginger.

She nods carefully.

"I'll bring you some flowers. We can plant them in these pots." I tell her good-bye and that I'll see her soon, and just as I reach the sidewalk she calls out:

"I like your shoes."

I know she does; she must have looked at my feet a dozen times today.

I don't want to leave her, not that I ever do, but today it's worse. Today he's here.

I remember what happened in our house when my father returned from his trips. That mounting panic we all felt knowing he was on his way. My mother would become quiet and distracted. Barbara would escape to a friend's house. Bett and I would head for the woods and linger there til the last possible minute, til dusk and dinnertime forced us home.

He wasn't violent, wasn't a drunkard—I don't remember him ever having a drink or even a glass of wine; he was very careful about what he ingested, never wanting to compromise his perfect looks, his brilliant mind.

No, he was a more cunning sort of bully. Charming and brutal at once. "Come here," he'd say with a smile, and we'd come. And then he'd tell us that our legs were getting fat or our skin looked oily or our clothes weren't right. "Go fix yourself," he used to say.

I remember the late night fights he and my mother had and how they terrified me. I remember her sobbing in the hallway and him explaining in a calm, clear voice that she repulsed him.

How different they are, my father and Ginger's. But that's the way it is with monsters. You can't tell them by sight. They can walk right by you and you wouldn't know.

TWELVE

The fog this morning is dense and wet. This is one of those days when it burns off at 1:00 and rolls back in at 3:00. As if submitting to the dismal weather, people on the street look forlorn, ill-fated, and in the space of one block I pass a one-legged pigeon, a one-armed man and two paraplegics. Not that wheelchairs are an uncommon sight in Berkeley; with curb cuts and ramps everywhere you look, this town is an oasis for the disabled. It reminds me of that Rudolf the Reindeer movie where all the broken toys are sent to an island for misfits. That's what Berkeley is: a place that takes in anyone.

I arrive at the Brick Hut several minutes early (another mania of mine) and grab the only available table, one unfortunately next to the door. Now I'm going to look over-eager, which I'm not.

Who can blame me, after the Jules fiasco? This is not the way to find a mate. It makes far more sense to shop for one, like they do at the marina Safeway in San Francisco. When I first heard that people were picking each other up in a grocery store, I was amused, incredulous, but then I started thinking about the way I browse people's carts while I'm waiting in line—don't we all?—and how intrigued I get when I see a bunch of arugula, or Parma prosciutto, or a gooey French cheese like Brin d'Amour: I'm half in love by then. The library is another good bet. One time I actually followed a woman for three blocks just because she'd checked out a Jean Rhys novel and a collection of short stories by Margaret Atwood. I should have struck up a conversation; I should have tried something, but I just let her round a corner and disappear.

Frankly I'm surprised that I spent so much time choosing an outfit—salmon-colored shirt, khaki pants, my best earrings; I even dabbed on a little perfume and mascara. Evidently I'm more hopeful than I feel.

I scan the crowd, looking for a blonde-haired woman waiting by herself. No such person, just couples and groups, women talking earnestly, women laughing. This place is like a private club—not that men aren't allowed; they just know to stay away. I used to denounce this sort of exclusivity, a long long time ago.

I can't help it, I keep looking at the door. The hardest thing about blind dates is managing that initial disappointment. I'm pretty good at pretense—shamelessly good—so I'm not so much afraid of my own reaction as I am my date's. If she's the honest, straightforward type and I prove to be a let down, well there it'll be, all over her face. Oh, she'll try to hide it, being kind—too late.

I see her before she sees me, through the window, so I have time to let my face do what it wants. I know it's her by the hair and the tan—Rita raved about both.

She's more attractive than I figured, taller too. I take in her face—nothing alarming there—then her body. She has a sturdy build: broad shoulders, solid thighs. I have no trouble imagining her hoisting 10-gallon trees and wheelbarrows of steer manure, an image bolstered by the outfit she's wearing: jeans, a light blue shirt, denim jacket and shoes that look like boots without the tops.

She swings open the door and, surprised to find me so fast, nearly stumbles. I smile in verification and what I see on her face is pure relief—unless she's as artful as I am.

"Lorrie?" she says.

"You must be Sharon." I stand up and shake her hand—her grip is strong—and immediately apologize.

"Sorry about the lousy table—it was the only one left."

"It's fine," she says, pulling out the other chair. She sits down, smiles at me. Nice teeth.

"Rita told me about your hair," she says. "It's really striking."

"Thank you. She mentioned yours too." I study Sharon's fine, lush hair, its depths of gold. "You *do* have great hair."

"Thanks," she says, blushing. Her eyes are slightly hooded, which I like. Late 30s is my guess.

I take a breath, begin.

"Rita tells me you work with plants."

She nods. "At the Wild Iris. I love it—it's so much better than where I was." And she tells me about the massive home improvement center in Hayward where she worked for six years and how corporate it was, how dull the inventory. The

Wild Iris, she tells me, specializes in unusual varieties—ornamental grasses, dwarf trees, water plants. "And our statuary is amazing. You should come by."

I will, I tell her, disclosing my own passion for plants. I tell her about the herb and vegetable garden I planted at Elba, which brings up the subject of cooking.

"Rita told me you're a fantastic cook. It must be fun," she says, "being a chef. So creative."

"It's alright," I say. This isn't the time for candor.

The waitress comes then, an aggressively homely woman with a shaved head, bad skin and earrings in the shape of double-sided hatchets. She pulls out her pad, regards us with ill-concealed impatience. I don't need to look at a menu; I get the same breakfast every time: two eggs over easy, homefries, rye toast and coffee. Sharon orders a bowl of oatmeal, a side of fruit and skim milk. Immediately my interest plummets. A health nut. It could be worse, I remind myself, instead of a prudent breakfast she could have ordered something inexcusable. Scrambled eggs cooked hard.

Our livelihoods out of the way, we begin the swapping of family data. Sharon is from Michigan and moved to California when her father, a research chemist, was transferred to a company in San Jose. Having lived in the south bay for "way too long," she decided last Christmas to start a new life here. "It's so freeing," she tells me, "the whole Berkeley thing."

The waitress slides our plates onto the table and I glance up at her and say thank you.

"Anything else?" she snaps. I look at her ravaged, hostile face and my sympathy dissolves. *Don't blame us.*

We shake our heads and she wheels away. There's a black tattoo on her calf but she's gone before I can see what it is.

I study my plate. The melon wedge looks fresh but the strawberry, two days too old, is bleeding into the potatoes, which are pale and sodden, not crusty like they should be. This is what you get when you learn how to cook: more and more chances to be disappointed. I pierce a yolk with my fork and the deep orange color gratifies me.

"So. Rita tells me you live on Hearst?"

Sharon stirs some brown sugar into her oatmeal. "Yeah, it's pretty nice. From the kitchen I have a view of the hills." She looks up. "How long have you lived in Berkeley?"

"Eight years."

"In the same place?"

"Oh no. When I first came here I lived in a house with three other women." I pick up a piece of toast, chuckle. "I remember the interview. The first thing they wanted to know was my astrological sign. Then they told me I couldn't bring any meat into the house or wear perfume. I lasted five months."

"Then what?"

"Then I got an apartment off Shattuck and stayed there for about three years, til I met Rita and moved into her place in Oakland. But the neighborhood got too noisy and we heard about this cute cottage for rent on Dana, so we ended up coming back here." I spear a hunk of potato. "She moved out last April."

Sharon looks at me with sympathy and I lift a shoulder, indicating my recovery.

"It's good you can still be friends," she says. "I could never do that with Greta."

Here it comes, the real reason Sharon moved up here.

"Who's Greta?" I ask, arching my eyebrows in innocence.

Sharon scoops some oatmeal onto her spoon, holds it over the bowl.

"We were together for eight years."

Oh no, I think, don't tell me she died.

"Then I caught her sweet-talking someone else on the phone." She flashes me another grin and brings the spoon to her mouth. "I'm over it now, mostly. But we're far from friends."

Recalling Jules's agonizing saga, I'm impressed by this tidy summary, and taking a sip of coffee I look at Sharon with fresh interest.

"What do you do when you're not working?" I ask. "I mean, what do you do for fun?"

She shrugs. "I run everyday."

I nod as if this makes sense to me.

"I like concerts," she says. "I go to Freight and Salvage a lot, and the Greek Theater. I don't do the bar scene though—I don't drink."

Egads. An oatmeal-eating, non-drinking jogger. I can feel the chasm widening.

I know what Rita will say. That I'm too critical, that there's nothing wrong with a woman who takes care of herself and if I have a problem with that, then maybe I need to take a look at own lifestyle, and she's right. I suppose. But there's something else about this woman, a quirk that's driving me nuts: she keeps smiling—not in a constant, dopey way; it comes out of nowhere, mid-sentence, for no reason. *What?* I keep thinking. What *is* it? As soon as I start to reciprocate, gamely, hopefully, the smile is gone; I settle back down and it pops up again. It's a tiring business, believe me.

("So she smiles a lot," Rita will say. "Is that so bad? *You* don't smile enough.")

She visits her family often, Sharon tells me, says she can't imagine living far away from them.

"Your whole family is back east, right?" she says. "Isn't it hard, being way out here?"

I assure her that it is.

She starts asking more questions about my family—where do they live, what do they do—and I'm amazed by my answers, by the ease with which a person can be dispatched: My mother, a divorcee who moved to Florida and now works in the billing department of a large construction company; Barbara, a respiratory therapist and mother of two who makes her home in Connecticut; Bett, single and living in rural Virginia. True enough, these descriptions—why do they sound like lies?

As always I omit my father. Talking about him feels too risky. Like walking under a ladder, or on a grave.

We finish our breakfast long before the waitress notices, and as the streaks of egg yolk harden on my plate Sharon talks about the business she hopes to start: organic herbs and vegetables, along with an assortment of natural soils and affordable pots. You can't go wrong with that, I tell her, and, encouraged, she launches into the particulars, how much space she'll need and where this nursery should be and what kind of vehicle she should purchase, and at some point I lean back and stop listening.

I look at her eyes and her mouth, and idly, amusing myself, I try to imagine her in my bed, her head on the other pillow. Rita and I used to spend hours laying in bed studying each other's face—of course we were in love back then and delighted with every freckle we found. That's what I miss the most: not the company, not the passion; I miss that place, that sweet oblivion. There's no respite out here.

She might sell edible flowers too, Sharon is saying—do I think there's a market for them? Would restaurants buy them? Absolutely, I nod, noticing how large her hands are. She isn't wearing any make-up or jewelry, which intrigues me, and I like her crow's feet, white against her dark tan, and the way her clear blue eyes seem lit from within.

But there it is again, that weird damn smile jumping out at me. My own mouth hardens and I have to force myself not to frown.

After that all I can see are reasons why I shouldn't bother with a second date. For one thing, she's talking too much; I'm getting bored with her business plans. For another thing she can't seem to tell I'm bored, even though I've been shifting in my chair, letting my gaze slide around the room. Not until our waitress shows up does Sharon stop yammering about leases and box vans and natural pest control.

"All set?" the waitress says, yanking our plates off the table.

"I think so," Sharon says. She looks at me for confirmation and I shrug and nod. Quick as a snake bite the waitress slaps our bill on the table; both of us reach for it.

"I'll get this," she says and I shake my head.

"I will. Mine costs more anyway."

"I'll leave the tip." She reaches for the leather satchel at her feet.

"Are you kidding? You're going to leave a tip?"

"I always leave a tip."

"Even when the service is this bad?"

"Well, they don't make much money," she explains, her voice soft with mercy, tinged with admonishment.

And that, on top of her smiling and her talking, would have been enough, but then I saw the book in her bag—a glossy paperback with a unicorn on the cover—and I couldn't get away from her fast enough.

I'm tying on my apron and reading the menu when Ann comes up and tells me she'll clean the flounder. Confused, I look again at the fish choices and see that the flounder is a saute dish tonight—why is she volunteering to prep my food? Then I hear her humming and I really get suspicious.

I follow her out to the grill station and watch as she swings her cleaver and the fish's head goes spinning off her cutting board and onto the floor. Flounders have both eyes on one side; looking down I feel doubly accused.

"What's new with you?" I ask.

"Not much." Smug, trying to fight back a smile, she picks up a filet knife and slits open the flounder's side. "I'm going to Greece in September."

Ah—her aunt has come through again. Last year Ann's aunt sent her to Provence, and before that, it was Portugal. This woman, who is childless, lives in a huge home in the Oakland hills and evidently enjoys throwing her money Ann's way.

"What part?" As if I know anything about Greece.

"The Cyclades."

She grins at me then, full force. If I were her I'd be spending that money on my teeth.

"Two weeks," she says, goading me.

"That's great," I lie. "Take lots of pictures."

She rolls her eyes at this, letting me know I've said something inane.

I walk back through the swinging doors just as Zee comes into the kitchen. Her cheeks and forehead are covered with Calamine.

"Oh Zee," I say. "Do you have it all over?"

"No. Just my arms and face, my hands too."

"Your hands? How can you work?"

She pulls off her bike helmet and stows it on the shelf above the pantry table, then bends down and unbuckles the leather straps on her ankles.

"It's okay—I'll just wear gloves."

I open the reach-in and, bracing myself for the weekend casualties, begin my kitchen triage. The smoked trout and roasted tomatoes are okay, but I have to dump the slick grey chunks of amberjack and at least a pound of mushy squid. And there's something else in here—something I haven't found yet—that smells so bad I'll have to take it all the way out to the dumpster.

"Do you know where you got it?" I ask, gingerly lifting another lid.

"Lake Anza, I guess—we hiked there on Friday. Do you know if we have any of those surgical gloves left?"

"I don't think we do. I'll call Molly—she can pick some up at Freeman's."

"I'll just use rubber gloves for now." Zee walks over to the sink and I see that she's still favoring her foot.

"This hasn't been your month," I tell her.

She turns to me, points to my arm. "Or yours," she smiles. "Or Juan's. We're the walking wounded."

She's right, I realize, thinking about the three of us, bandaged and limping, preparing ourselves for another assault. Even our lexicon implies battle: we "fire" food; get "buried" under tickets. I look around the kitchen, at the ruined Hobart mixer, the duct-taped leg on the panty table, the wet wad of towels wrapped around the faucet, the water puddling beneath it on the cast iron stove. Behind that wall is the free world, eating and drinking in a room filled with flowers, never dreaming their gorgeous food was born in these soggy trenches.

It's the kind of night we pray for, slow and steady, without mishap, and when it's over we feel victorious. I even get what amounts to a medal—a glass of champagne sent to me by a patron who loved his alfredo. It's a gesture for which I'm inordinately grateful, and what that says about my life and expectations is something I'd rather not ponder.

There wasn't any leftover steak tonight so I brought Murphy a chunk of flounder. Out of politeness he takes three or four bites, then leaves the rest in his bowl as a quiet reminder that mammals are more to his liking.

Wine in hand I sink into the sofa and Murphy jumps up and lays down alongside my thigh. Frowning, I watch a red and blue male guppy swimming around the baby tank; he wants to eat the fry that were born yesterday. I have no idea where I'll house this latest brood—guppies give birth almost monthly—but I can't surrender them, I know that; probably I'll have to give up on guppies altogether.

Murphy sees something I don't, something near the ceiling. I watch his head move as he follows it from one corner to another, his tail gently flicking. I've observed this behavior in other cats and I've come to understand that what they are watching are ghosts. Dogs can hear things that people can't, but cats can see them, maybe because of their strange pupils. This isn't a rare occurrence and I'm not unduly disturbed by it; still I'm jolted by the ringing of the phone. Who could be calling me at this hour?

"Hello?"

"Lorrie?"

"Bett!"

"Hi. How come you're never home? I called you like three times tonight and I kept getting your stupid machine."

"Bett, I work at night. I told you."

"Spook died."

Spook? Oh—the dog.

"What happened to him?"

"Some asshole hit him. Last night. They didn't even stop and pull him off the road." She starts crying then. "Lorrie, he was such a good dog. You know? Real friendly."

And I have started crying too, for Bett, and Spook, and everything else in this world that doesn't stand a chance. Just once I wish she could get a break.

"How old was he?"

"Oh he was young, not even two, I don't think. He still acted like a puppy, you know? He'd get down on his front paws and wag his tail." I hear her inhale; she's smoking again. "He used to steal my shoes. He'd run around the cabin with my sandal in his mouth. He didn't bark, though—I guess because he was deaf." Her voice breaking, she adds, "Lorrie, he couldn't hear the car coming."

"Oh Bett," I murmur, my tears shifting and blurring the cupboard in front of me. "I wish I could be there with you." I pause, helpless. "I don't know what to say to make you feel better."

And Bett, in her fashion, rallies at this, tells me it's okay, that she'll be fine, that she knows it'll take time and not to worry, that she didn't mean to make me feel bad, and I tell her I am so glad she called, that I've really been wanting to talk to her.

"Where are you calling from, anyway?"

"I'm over at Rudy's."

"Who's Rudy?"

"He lives in a house across the road from my cabin. He's really nice. He helped me get a snake out of the bathroom last week."

"There was a *snake* in your bathroom?"

"Rudy told me it was a hognose. You should have seen this thing. It *hissed* at us!"

"Jesus. How did you get rid of it?"

"Rudy caught it with a stick and we put it in a bag and let it go in the woods. Hognose snakes aren't poisonous. Rudy says you can tell if a snake is harmless if it has round pupils, but I told him, who's going to get that close?"

"What does Rudy do? For work, I mean."

"He doesn't work—he's on disability. He lost an arm and one eye in a well-digging accident."

"That's awful."

"He used to live with his mother, but she died a couple years ago, and then he had the accident."

Good god. This is just the sort of hard-luck person Bett would attract.

"So, do you like him?" I ask. "Are you dating?"

Bett gives a raspy chuckle.

"Lorrie, he's like *sixty*. He's my buddy."

I'm thrilled to hear that Bett has a buddy and I tell her so. "You know, I've been worried about you."

"Lorrie, you're *always* worried about me."

"Yeah, I know, but it's been so long since I've seen you, and you just keep moving farther away, and you don't have a phone, and, I don't know, I just worry that you're lonely."

"I'm fine," she tells me. "Sometimes I get lonely but I have Rudy, and I might get another dog. Sylvia—she owns the laundromat—her dog just had puppies. They're so cute, they're part St. Bernard and part German shephard and something else. They're free."

I'll bet they are. What about the shots, the neutering, the cost of feeding a dog that big—these are things I don't bother to mention: there's never been much point in cautioning Bett. And so I ask her about Burkes Pond and what it's like living there, and she tells me about the post office ("the size of a toll booth") and the market that used to be a stable. "There's still hay poking out of the corners," she laughs, "and all you can buy are things like Wonderbread and Spaghettios. And baby food, they have a lot of that. And beer and bait. They have milk too but it's always expired."

"What about produce?"

"Lorrie, people don't buy that kind of stuff here, they grow their own. Rudy's always giving me green beans and carrots and peas. Next month he'll have corn."

She's eating fresh vegetables, that's something. I ask her how she likes working at the marina and she tells me she doesn't.

"They pee in the boats. And it's not the men, it's the women; they forget to bring a can and they don't want to get in the water, so they just pee in the boat. It's gross. They leave everything in the boats—beer cans, pieces of watermelon, soggy sandwiches, bait. But I only have two more months—they close up after Labor Day."

"What are you going to do then?"

"I don't know. I can probably get a job in Quincy—that's like 15 minutes from here. Rudy says he can drive me there, but I can't ask him to do that, and anyway his truck is really old."

I hop off the counter where I've been sitting and start pacing around the kitchen.

"Why don't you come here? There are plenty of jobs here and you could live with me as long as you need to."

I hear her exhale a stream of smoke. "Lorrie. I couldn't live where you live, with all those people and cars."

This is not the first time we've talked about this. She's right, this isn't her kind of place. A few months after I moved to California Bett visited me—her first and last time (she vows) on a plane—and while she liked the ocean and the views, she said she'd go crazy if she had to live here.

And so I let it go. I lean back against the countertop and twist the phone cord between my fingers and try to picture Bett on her end of the line.

"Are you in Rudy's kitchen?"

"Nope. I pulled the phone out on the porch."

"Where's Rudy?"

"He's watching True Grit." And she makes me laugh then by doing a perfect imitation of John Wayne.

"I miss you," I tell her, my smile fading.

"I miss you too," she says.

She tells me again about the snake in her bathroom and I realize that she's inebriated. Bett can drink a lot (she's one of those all or nothing drinkers) and her tolerance is amazing; the only way I can tell she's been drinking is by the way she repeats herself.

"What are you looking at right now?" I ask. "The lake?"

I hear the flick of her lighter.

"No, I'm looking at a moth on the screen door—it's huge. We have a lot of moths here. You know luna moths, with those big green wings? Last night I followed two of them all the way down Main Street."

I can see those marvelous moths floating down the road and Bett, delighted, pursuing them. She's always loved the night—stars and fireflies, frogs and crickets. It's only when she's indoors that Bett fears the dark.

"I'm trying to learn the names of all the moths and butterflies," she says. "Rudy has a book on insects."

I remember then the books I sent her.

"Hey, did you ever get that Larry McMurtry collection I sent you?"

"Yeah, oh yeah. I did. Thanks."

"Well? Did you like them?"

"Um, you know, I'm not quite *through* them. I read them a little at a time. They're good, though."

"You used to read a book in one day," I can't help saying.

"I know," she sighs. "But I can't sit still like that anymore, I get jittery."

Jittery?

"And part of it is my eyes," she says. "I lost one of my contacts so I have to wear my glasses and they're pretty scratched up."

"Bett. You need to get new contacts—or new glasses. How long has it been since you've had your eyes checked? Is there an eye doctor in town?"

"There's one in Quincy," she says. "Don't worry, I'll get new glasses." A pause. "*I will.*" And then, deflecting any further investigation, she asks what's new with me.

"Not much, still working at the restaurant. But I met a little girl—her name is Ginger. She's the greatest kid, Bett; she looks just like you."

"Poor thing," she laughs.

I don't mention Ginger's father. I just talk about how smart she is and how much I like reading to her. Bett gets very quiet then and I start to wonder if I've made her sad, if all this talk about Ginger has made her think about children and her own failed pregnancies, and so I change the subject. I tell her about my burn, the only other news I have to offer.

"Burns are awful," she agrees. "You should see the scars on Rudy's arm—the one he still has."

She needs to get off the phone, she says, or she'll be owing Rudy her whole paycheck.

"Call me collect next time," I tell her, though I know she won't, "and take care," I add, futilely.

She hangs up the phone and I lose her again.

THIRTEEN

Joel and I are tying red silk flowers onto his marijuana plants. This is a precaution, an attempt to fool any airborne authorities. We have no idea if this ploy is effective but we figure it can't hurt.

Long pungent buds are forming on the plants and our hands absorb the skunky odor as we fasten fake zinnias onto the branches. Joel, cheerful as always, is singing Hotel California. He sings without shame, his voice strong and clear, slightly off-key; when he reaches a verse he can't remember he supplies his own words and the startling lyrics amuse me. I wonder sometimes if I'm not a little bit in love with Joel; it's possible, I suppose, though I don't believe my interest is romantic. I think it's the *idea* of Joel that attracts me, the reassurance he provides. On those days when their crimes weigh too heavily, when I can barely muster enough forgiveness to even look at a man, it helps to consider Joel.

When we're finished here we're going over to Ginger's; I bought some petunias and marigolds for the pots on her porch and Joel has offered to give me a ride.

"I really appreciate your helping me out today," I say when he comes to the end of his song.

"Sure." He turns to face me and for a moment I bask in his cool green gaze. "It's nice, the time you spend with that kid."

I smile at him. "Thanks. You know, you're the only one who's said that? Everyone else thinks I should keep my distance."

"Why?"

"They think I'm going to get hurt." I frown, twist another wire. "Like that's a good reason to abandon her." The word makes me stop and think. That's what it would amount to now: abandonment. On what day, at what point, did I become capable of causing more harm than good?

"What do *you* think?" I ask him.

Joel turns back to his plants and says exactly what I knew he would say: "I don't think you should worry about it." This is surfer's wisdom and Joel's standard advice. "Do what makes you happy," he shrugs.

Happy. It's an option I keep forgetting.

On the way to Ginger's I tell Joel about the drawing class I found for Shirley.

"It's perfect. It meets every Tuesday and Thursday morning, which means I get to look after Ginger. Today's her first class. She's missed a couple but they're letting her in anyway."

Joel swings onto Shattuck and immediately we're stopped in traffic. "Is she any good?" he asks.

"No, not really. But I'm hoping it'll boost her self-esteem, make her feel important. I'm sure her creepy husband isn't thrilled about it, but who cares?"

The light changes and Joel accelerates. I smile out the window. "Wait til you see how excited she is about this class—she even bought a special outfit to wear today." I've told Joel all about Shirley and I turn now to watch his expression. "A new halter top with matching shorts."

"Far out," he nods.

Ginger is mesmerized by Joel; I knew she would be. She looks right past me as we come up the walk and fastens her eyes on him. I don't even think she notices the flowers in my hands.

"Ginger," I say when we reach the porch—she is sitting on the steps—"this is my friend Joel."

Joel sets the buckets, trowels and soil next to one of the clay pots, then bends down and shakes Ginger's hand.

"Very happy to meet you," he tells her earnestly.

Immediately she grins and lowers her chin to her chest.

"Don't be rude," Shirley says, "*say* something." She is standing behind the screen door.

We all turn and look at her. She is wearing her new ensemble, a bright red halter top, and short-shorts, with yellow polka dots; her midriff is showing and the skin is pasty and slack, swelling over the too-tight waistband.

Joel stands up and, seeing how handsome he is, Shirley straightens her shoulders and, hiding the hand that's holding a cigarette, reaches for her hair with the other.

"This is Joel," I say, and turning to him, "This is Shirley, Ginger's mother."

"Hi!" he says brightly. She stares at him, caught for a moment in that heartbreak smile of his, then stammers an apology, says she hasn't had time to fix her hair. Ginger eyes her mother's hair in puzzlement and I fight back a smile.

"Well, I should be going," says Joel. "Have fun planting your flowers," he tells Ginger.

"Okay," she squeaks.

"Nice to meet you," he says to Shirley.

She clears her throat. "Yeah, um, you too."

We all study him as he jogs down the walk and when he reaches the street I call out, "Thanks, Joel!" He waves and gets into the van, and Shirley, watching him regretfully, blows a long stream of smoke out the screen.

I set down the flower packs and point to the pots. "You mind, Shirley, if we plant some flowers in these?" She stares at me a moment, her mind still on Joel, then shrugs and turns away.

"Help yourself."

The first thing I do is pick up Barbie, who has fallen from the dead ficus and is lying face down and naked on the grey dirt, one arm stretched over her head. Judging by the tan and sky blue eye shadow, this one must be Malibu Barbie, or whatever they call her these days. Not much has changed: she still has pointy breasts, a freakishly small waist and heels that never touch the earth. Bald and smudged, her lipstick gone, her toes chewed off, this Barbie is a long way from Malibu.

I push her tired arm down to her side. "Is this your doll?" I ask Ginger. She shakes her head.

"Where did it come from?"

"I don't know. It's been here for a long time," she nods.

"Do you like Barbie dolls?"

She makes a face, shakes her head again.

"I didn't either," I tell her.

It's true. Dolls bored me; I didn't understand them. I wanted cap guns and cowboy hats, microscopes and sea monkeys. It was my mother who, in an effort perhaps to reshape my destiny, foisted Barbie on me. I didn't know what to do with her; she couldn't even bend. All she could do was lean up against the vinyl wall of her livingroom, which was also her carrying case, and wait for someone to change her clothes. Her life was pointless. Hoping to nudge my homemaking instincts, my mother redoubled her efforts and bought me a Ken doll. He only made things worse. I couldn't respect Ken: he had no skills, no life apart from Barbie. Once or twice I pressed them against each other but it didn't work for them and it didn't work for me. Not until my friend Sara left her Prom Barbie at my house one day did the game become interesting. My doll was the Malibu model, the most popular one at the time. She was the more daring, I decided, of the two, and not at all embarrassed when I made her kiss Prom Barbie. They both enjoyed this and so I laid them down. There they were, their eyes locked in amazement, shy Barbie in her scratchy pink dress, reaching upward, and bold Barbie, in a red bathing suit, poised on tip toes above her. Ken was completely useless after that and I forgot all about him.

Ginger doesn't want the doll and so I slip her into my backpack where she can enjoy a few hours of hard-earned privacy. At some point I will wrap a cloth or newspaper around her and put her in the trash, and eventually she'll end up at a dump surrounded by legions of other lost dolls whose hard plastic bodies will not let them leave this earth.

Pulling out the ficus feels like an act of mercy. It comes out easily, gratefully, the roots a mummified clump the size of my fist. There is nothing in the other pot but three crushed beer cans. I remove these and hand Ginger a bucket and trowel.

"You can dig the dirt out of that pot while I do this one," I tell her. Put the dirt in the bucket and then we'll dump it behind the bushes."

"Why do have to take out the dirt?"

"Because we need to put in good fresh soil so the flowers will grow."

She gives me an aggrieved look. "What if I find a *worm*?"

"You won't."

She sighs and starts scooping. "I don't even like dirt," she mutters, her words barely audible. I ignore this and she adds, more adventurously, "At all."

This makes me smile and I have to turn my back so she doesn't see. Pushing my trowel into the crusted soil, I suddenly remember the white cat that was sleeping in this pot the day I met Ginger.

"Hey—do you have a cat?"

"No. My mom says, 'NO PETS.' I can't even have a goldfish." She pauses. "Do you *believe* that?"

This is one of Ginger's new catch phrases, always accompanied by an exaggerated look of disapproval. 'What in the *world*?' is another recent favorite.

"Who owns that white cat I saw here?"

"I don't know," she says. "He used to come here to sleep but my father scared him away with a stick. He *hates* cats."

I yank up a trowelful of dirt with such fury that it flies out of the pot and onto the porch.

"Do you get along with your father?" It's a pointless question to ask a child but I can't help myself.

"What's this?" Ginger dangles something green in front of my face and I jerk back.

"Half a tennis ball," I tell her, regaining my balance.

"Yuck," she says and tosses it into the yard.

"That's trash," I tell her. "It needs to go in the trash can."

"I was going to put it in the trash *after*."

"Ah," I nod. "After." I look at her bucket. "You're almost done. You're going to beat me."

She eyes my pail, digs faster.

"Is your father ever mean to you?" Out of the corner of my eye I see her small shoulders lift.

"Sometimes he yells."

"At you?"

"Sometimes at me and sometimes at my mom." She turns around, beams at me.

"Look!" she says. "I beat you."

Sure enough the pot is empty—aside from a few cigarette butts—and I shake my head in amazement.

"That means you get to decide what flowers go where."

The screen door swings open and Shirley steps out on the porch. She has put on lipstick and too much blusher, and her wild red hair, most of it, is bunched inside a fuzzy yellow tie.

"You look nice," I tell her.

She grins, embarrassed, and her broken front tooth comes into view.

"At least I match," she says, pointing first to her hair tie, then to the polka dots, then to her plastic sandals. I nod approvingly.

"Yellow looks good on you."

"It's our favorite color," Ginger says.

"I know."

Shirley hurries down the steps and I reel for a moment in the bank of her cologne, something dense and floral. I am a child again, back on those wooden floors in Woolworths, fingering the tiny perfumes. Blue Velvet. Evening in Paris.

"Shirley?"

She turns around, impatient.

"Do you mind if I take Ginger to Caspar's for lunch?"

"Go ahead," she says, flicking her hand in a gesture of dismissal. She points to her daughter. "You be good." Shirley heads for the Galaxie and Ginger rolls her eyes at me.

"She always says that."

Ginger is eager to plant the flowers and immediately reaches for the first marigold I take out of the pack.

"Wait," I tell her. "We have to disturb the memory."

Her forehead rumples. "Disturb the *memory?*"

"The memory of the roots." I pull at the webbing of white fibers. "See that? If we don't break up the roots, they'll keep going around and around; they won't know they can grow bigger." I pull out another marigold and hand it to her. "You try it."

She hesitates, then picks at one little piece of root and immediately winces, looks up at me in fear, and I see how many times she's been stopped, blamed, and for the second time today I am shot through with rage.

"That's *perfect,*" I tell her. "Just do that a little bit more."

Slowly, eyeing me over her glasses, Ginger finishes picking at the roots and I hand her another marigold. She is very meticulous and it takes her a long time to plant all the flowers I bought. At one point she puts a blue petunia alongside a red petunia, then decides it will be lonely for the the other blue petunias and pulls it out. There are several of these mistarts before she's satisfied and I have to force myself more than once not to interfere.

"There," she announces when she has tucked the last flower in the soil. She grins at me, delighted with herself. Her arms are dirty up to elbows, her face is shiny with effort, and her flyaway hair is damp and tangled. I grin back.

"Now we have to water them. Do you have a hose?"

She points behind the bushes to my right. "I think it's down there."

I walk down the steps and peer through the stunted brown shrubbery. Sure enough there's a cheap hose half buried in leaves; it's not easy to get to and I break several dry branches trying. I finally manage to drag out the limp coil and thread it behind the other bushes alongside the porch so that Ginger has easier access to it next time.

"You have to water these everyday," I tell her.

"I know," she says, taking the hose from me, "or they'll die."

We stand back and survey our work and Ginger tells me the flowers are "really really pretty." I tilt my head, trying to see what she does. Frail is how they look to me. Frail and brave.

It's already past noon and if we're going to go to Caspar's we need to get a move on. Thrilled at the prospect of an outing, Ginger flies up the steps to get her shoes. "And wash your hands," I call out as the screen door slams.

I turn off the water, frowning at a dark greasy circle in the dirt where Ginger's father must be dumping his used oil. There are more tires now and I wonder why he's stacking them in front of the garage door and not on the side. The garage is in worse shape than the house; most of the paint has flaked off and there are holes near the roof where the wood has rotted away. I'd like to see what's behind that warped door and I walk around the corner, looking for a side entrance with a window in it. I find one, but the glass is covered with a thick coat of black paint; it looks fresh. Above the door knob, hanging from a rusted hasp, is a big shiny padlock. The newness of it chills me. What is he up to?

"I'm ready," says Ginger. There are two wet marks on her dress where she has half-dried her hands. On her feet are those floppy white sandals, which make me remember the sneakers I want to buy her.

I glance at the side door again, at the the ridged brush strokes covering the glass, the jagged black edges where he overpainted.

"What's in your garage?" I ask, lightly, as we walk back toward the porch.

She shrugs. "I don't know, I can't go in there. It's my *father's* garage."

"Should we leave your father a note and tell him where we went?"

"Why?"

"Because won't he be worried if he comes home and you're not here?"

Ginger shakes her head. "I don't think he's coming home today."

"I think I'll leave a note just in case."

Ginger follows me into the house. As usual the place smells like cigarettes and the kitchen is a jumble of unwashed dishes. Shirley's sketch pad is open on the table and I pause to study her progress: the penguins are disproportionately small, and there is a fantastic number of starfish now clinging to the rock, but all in all, it's not a bad attempt. On the sofa is a pile of laundry, which Shirley has started to fold, and a magazine. I come closer and see a man in camouflage scowling from the cover, his thick hands around an assault rife. On the pinto carpet are two more gun magazines, a Slim Jim wrapper and a red matchbook with black lettering: Big Willy's—A Store for Adults. I turn it over and find the address, some place in Long Beach, and the buxom profile of a nude woman. I wonder if he dropped it accidentally or left it here on purpose—god knows he's mean enough. "Jerk," I mutter, slipping it into my backpack, worried that Ginger has already seen it.

I wash my hands in the kitchen, then spend a couple minutes stacking the dishes in the sink: if Ginger's father does come home I don't want him seeing the kitchen like this—that won't help any of us.

"C'mon," Ginger pleads. She is fiddling with a loose strip of Formica on the edge of the counter, pulling it up and letting it flap back down.

"Give me one minute." I find a pen sticking out from under the coffeemaker and look around for something to write on. There's nothing on the counter but bills and flyers. "Do you have any paper?"

She runs into her bedroom and comes out with a piece of pink construction paper. I ponder the wording a moment and decide that the less said, the better.

Mr. Hebert—Hi. Ginger and I have gone to Caspar's for lunch. We'll be right back. Lorrie Rivers.

I read it through one more time and add, fatuously, an exclamation point after the Hi. Looking up then, at the table, the livingroom, the open front door, I am filled with foreboding.

"Let's go," I say, taking Ginger's hand.

Twice on the way to Caspar's we're approached by homeless people wanting change. The first is a black man with haunted eyes and matted gray hair who wordlessly holds out his hand. The second is a young woman pushing an over-stuffed shopping cart. She is wearing a long dress, the hemline filthy from trailing the pavement, and is chanting profanities. She glares at me and demands a dollar; I shake my head and look away and she snarls some awful epithet.

Ginger stops, looks over her shoulder.

"C'mon," I urge. "Don't stare."

Sandals flapping, she catches up with me. "What's wrong with that lady?"

"She's sick. She's lost her mind."

"Why?"

"I don't know why."

"She should go to the doctor."

"She can't. She doesn't have any money."

Ginger falls silent at this and I wonder what conclusions she is drawing. I look down at her wispy hair, almost colorless in the noonday sun, and squeeze her hand reassuringly.

There's a line at Caspar's and as we wait Ginger counts the pigeons that are milling about, ogling the sidewalk for crumbs.

"Fourteen," she declares. "No—wait! Fifteen—no, *four*teen." She points to a pigeon on the curb. "Look at that one." He is smaller than the others and his feathers are dark and greasy-looking. Sidelined by the healthy birds, he is waiting for a miracle.

"Poor little guy," I murmur.

"I'm going to give him some of my bread," she says resolutely.

"That would be very nice." I study her profile, the rounded forehead, jutting chin, and my eyes brim with tears. The urgency in her, the fierce belief. How much of that will be lost?

I look away, concentrate on the large plastic menu board behind the counter.

"What do you want on your hot dog?"

"Mustard."

"Do you want any french fries or onion rings?"

"French fries."

"With catsup?"

"Yes," she says, then, proudly, raising her eyebrows, "*Please.*"

There's no place left to sit so we stand at the counter to eat our lunch. Ginger starts on her fries, pulling them out one by one, dipping both ends in the catsup. When we go to the aquarium, she tells me, we're going to see whales.

"Sharks, not whales."

"And those turtles that know where to go." She talks about the aquarium a lot, making sure I don't forget. This is the week I plan to ask Shirley for her permission, figuring by now I've proven my harmlessness. There's a chance she'll want to come with us—I've prepared myself for that.

Looking at me sideways Ginger pulls her hot dog out of the bun and, attempting to establish complicity, pushes the bread my way. "We need to save this," she nods, "for the birds."

Feigning disapproval, I frown at the bun a moment, then pick it up and tear it into two pieces.

"You give them half and I'll give them half."

It's not easy trying to feed the sick bird, but we manage at last by luring the other pigeons far enough away. "Here's more," Ginger chants as she tosses her crumbs to the scrawny creature, who most certainly gets his fill. On the way back home Ginger tells me that he said thank you.

"Oh? You heard him say thank you?"

She shakes her head. "*No.* He flapped his wings. That's how birds talk."

I love these easy explanations of hers, the way she comforts herself moment by moment. All children do, I suppose—god knows Bett fashioned enough fantasies.

The thought of Bett alarms me, brings with it something ominous, a winged shadow.

"Ginger," I begin, anxiously—this is something I've been wanting to talk about. "Do you know that I'm your friend? Do you know that you can tell me anything? If you're sad, or if you're scared, you can talk to me. Do you know that?"

She nods, tentative, and the sun glints off her glasses.

I tell her everything then, my heart beating wildly, in case no one else has. I don't care if it upsets her.

"If someone ever touches you that way, you just tell me. You tell me and I'll make them stop."

I can't see her face and I need to.

"Ginger." I bend down, cup her cheeks in my hands. "Do you understand?" And I see that she does.

She has turned away, won't look at me. She's not going to say a word.

And he knows it.

They don't tell you to keep it a secret; they're that sure you will.

There was only one time my father showed concern. We were in the backyard. Barbara was clipping grass along the patio; Bett, crouched beside the house, was trying to catch the crickets that scuttled across the cement foundation. My mother must have been inside; she was always, in these memories, somewhere else, a wall, a room, away.

My father, who had finished his projects for the day, was eyeing me from his chaise longue while I pulled weeds from our newly planted lawn. He was wearing a pair of black shorts, and no shirt, and his long tanned legs were crossed at the ankles.

"Why don't you take off your top?" he said with that teasing smile he sometimes used. I tried to ignore him and he asked again.

"Go ahead, take it off. You could use the sun."

I was Ginger's age at the time, still a child but just beginning to feel embarrassed about my body. I could feel my face getting warm.

"I don't want to."

"Why not?"

"I just don't, I really don't." I was pleading with him now. He did the same sort of thing at the beach, had us pull our bathing suit straps off our shoulders before he took pictures, said it made us look cuter.

"Oh come on, don't be such a wet rag—take it off."

I started to cry; there was nothing I could do. Wildly, in blind terror, I said something amazing, words I had never uttered before:

"I'll tell mom."

I wasn't sure what I meant and neither was he. His smile vanished and I saw his fear, just the edge of it, before his anger took over.

"You little bitch." His voice was cold, menacing.

I wanted to run; I couldn't breathe.

"Don't you ever EVER say that again."

I didn't. I was afraid of his wrath, but even more afraid of my secret. Now I knew how bad it was.

FOURTEEN

Cheerful as always, Joel whistles as he tosses two sleeping bags into the van. He and Sasha have decided, spontaneously, to head up to Lake Tahoe. Even she seems festive, though I suspect her excitement is related not to this getaway but to her latest victory: she just beat her best time on Grizzly Peak. I will bring in their mail, I assure them, and keep on eye on things, which means, as far as Sasha is concerned, the bikes.

Lake Tahoe. I remember my first trip there, with Elizabeth, just weeks after we met. It was in the winter, and dark by the time we arrived. I could hear the water lapping the shoreline, and I could smell the cold trees, but all I could see were shadows on darker shadows. Elizabeth had borrowed a friend's cabin for the weekend, a rustic little place with a potbellied stove and iron skillets hanging from the walls, and five minutes after we walked through the door we were sunk in her feather bed, making love in the moonlight that spilled from a window etched with ice. Eventually we pulled up the velvet quilt and I fell into the deepest sleep I've ever known. The first thing I saw when I opened my eyes the next morning was a row of icicles glistening in the window. I got out of bed, pulled back the half curtain—and gasped. There it was, a wide still lake, unimaginably blue, framed by snow-topped mountains, each one precisely reflected in its mirror surface. I looked at Elizabeth, still sleeping in that feather bed, and the cozy room with its pine walls and worn braided rug, and then I turned back to the window and gazed out for the longest time. Whatever blunders I'd made, however long my list of shortcomings, I had clearly been forgiven.

How long ago was that—seven years, eight? I have no idea what Elizabeth is doing now, nor do I care; no doubt the feeling, or lack of it, is mutual. Hearts. They just can't be trusted.

One time Kris and I drove to her parents place in Hawthorne, Nevada. It was a long drive through nothing but desert, and strewn along the flat roads was the wreckage of dashed dreams: junk cars, listing houses, sprung sofas, boarded-up stores. That's how I picture the love we discard, only tidier. If we could look behind us there would be a road, and here and there on both sides of this road would be boxes, brown paper-wrapped like UPS parcels; no postage, no address, just a name. Tony. Elizabeth. Kris. Rita.

Rita of course would like to believe that she is not among this lot, that I still burn a candle for her, the flame small but steady. I play along, a wink here, a smile there—why withhold what costs me nothing?

Thinking of Rita coincides with a message from her on my answering machine. She wants to come over tomorrow for breakfast—she'll bring bagels and fruit; how does 9:00 sound; call her if there's a problem. There is also a message from Barbara asking me to phone her when I get a chance. As usual her tone is rushed and businesslike; I can see her hanging up the wallphone, plucking her purse off the black marble counter and heading for the door, her mouth firm with purpose.

There is no time to sit with Murphy—I have to be at work in 15 minutes. Knowing I feel bad about this, he walks over to where I keep the canned catfood and lays one chunky orange paw on the cupboard. It's just a suggestion; even offended, Murphy is polite.

"Okay, buddy." I open a can of Friskies and fork out a small portion, just enough to tide him over til I come back tonight with real carnage.

There's a blue Saab parked behind the restaurant—Lewis must be working Ann's shift. Sure enough I find him perched on top of my reach-in when I come into the kitchen. As usual he is reading a book, his back pressed to the wall, his skinny knees drawn up to his chest. He will stay here for at least another half hour, then unfold himself, scan the menu and, with supreme indifference, prep exactly what he needs to get him through the evening. There will be nothing left for Ann tomorrow, not an ounce of fumet, not one tablespoon of aioli. Even if there is something left, he's sure to throw it out, I've seen him. And if you make the mistake of asking him why, he'll just blink at you a couple times and then shake his head, regretfully, as if your ignorance can't be helped. He'll tell you that the food can't possibly be served again. He'll use words like "ghastly" and "objectionable."

The thing is, Lewis thinks he's more evolved than the rest of us—maybe he is. Ann says he lives off a trust fund and has degrees in philosophy, classical literature and languages; I think he's still enrolled at UCB. Where he learned to cook, or why he deigns to work here, I can't imagine. He handles the orders alright, but he doesn't give a damn about food; all he wants to do is read, Proust, Beckett, Joyce—the sort of authors I keep giving up on. Last year when Ann was in Provence and he was covering for her, I mentioned my own interest in literature and he reached into his backpack and wordlessly shoved a book into my hands. It was a collection of poems by H.D., poems I spent several mornings trying to understand and never did. "These were great," I said when I gave him back the volume, and he nodded in solemn accord.

"Hi, Lewis."

He lifts his hand and I'm not sure if it's a greeting or a warning—he doesn't look up.

"No Ann tonight? Is she sick?"

He shakes his head and continues to read. It's just like him to offer the barest response possible.

"Are the menus done?"

This time I get a curt nod. Jerk, I think, vigorously, just in case he's telepathic.

Juan is on his knees cleaning the floor drains. He's wearing orange vinyl rubber gloves that come up to his elbows and goggles to protect his eyes against splashing bleach. For being such a macho guy, he is very concerned with personal safety.

"Hi, Juan."

He glances at me over the mound of his shoulder and I can tell by that stern, accusing look that this is one of his hostile days. Great. Molly must have asked him to do something extra, or maybe he's homesick and can't stand the sight of us. Frankly it's better when he comes in drunk, singing La Bamba and calling me senora and flashing those red-gummed, gold-toothed smiles.

Walking out into the diningroom I see Andre at the sideboard folding napkins. His hands move sharply, his back is ramrod straight. He glances up, greets me without a smile.

"What's wrong?" I ask him.

He frowns. "Ty."

I wait for the story.

"He got home last night from Reno. Lost some money—he won't say how much. And there's a big dent in the car."

"The Jaguar?"

Andre nods. "Naturally—you think Ty would have taken the Civic?" His hands stop moving. "And he's met someone." Andre looks at me, his dark-lashed eyes starting to tear. "Big surprise, huh?"

I never liked Ty, or any of the others Andre has fallen for. Unfortunately he has a weakness for younger men, the beautiful, callous variety. I reach out, cover Andre's hand with my own, and two tears roll down his long handsome face and onto the white linen. "Never again," he whispers bitterly. Which isn't true.

"I'm sorry, Andre."

He shakes his head, annoyed with himself. "Oh, it's fine," he says, snatching up another napkin. "It's not like I'm losing much, right?"

I nod, carefully, and offer him a brave sad smile, which he returns, and then I slide over to Molly's desk and pick up a menu. Roast duck breast. Fried fennel and calamari. Grilled monkfish brochettes. Hmm—Lewis better get busy.

My prep isn't too bad: gazpacho, panfried flounder with hazelnuts, penne with pesto and cherry tomatoes. I'll be ready by 4:00, or so I think. Then I open the walk-in.

A zoo is what it reminds me of, the reptile house, dark and clammy, oozing with beastly odors. Nothing has turned lethal yet, but everything is headed there; every animal smells too strong. I lift a towel and get a noseful of duck, lift another and inhale a flounder. There are mussels in the next tub, every one of them open and panting, their purply unctuous innards beginning to shrivel. Even the celery has a green reek.

I walk back into the kitchen and pick up the phone.

"The compressor went out," I tell Lewis as I'm dialing the repair service. He looks up from his book with mild interest and I wonder why anyone, especially anyone as homely as Lewis, would insist on wearing those big black glasses.

"I don't know when it died, but the temperature's close to 50. We have to get our food out of there and into the reach-ins."

Lewis, being Lewis, finishes the page he is reading before calmly swinging his legs off my reach-in. Tucking the book into his armpit, he strolls over to where I'm piling bodies onto the pantry table. The loss is greater than I thought. The mussels, we nod in unison, have to go, along with the squid, the duck, the tub of shucked oysters, the black gob of monkfish and the cloudy-eyed flounder. Only the New York strip, which we check with a thermometer, passes muster (and that's only because it's been sitting on the steel floor of the walk-in, which of course is a code violation. We are not afraid of health inspectors, no one is. Twice a year one of them shows up, gives us a long list of fix-its, then has a nice free lunch).

I suggest running a vegetarian menu tonight but Molly nixes the idea, not wanting to disappoint our flesh-eating patrons. Instead she stops at a grocery store on her way in and buys what they have: snapper, naturally; orange hunks of pre-cut salmon; tuna steaks—who knows what species; and ten frozen trout, fresh from the box, boned and splayed, hard as plywood, and as Lewis and I try to coax some flavor out of these sad offerings, Molly designs a new menu. I know how it'll read. The snapper will become Oregon coast rockfish, the salmon will hail from the Alaskan wilderness, and the trout I'm thawing under the faucet will have arrived this morning from Idaho. She will even name the river, which she will find in the atlas she keeps in her desk just for nights like this.

I dreamed I met a woman at a dinner party. She was pretty and blonde and very smart, and after the meal we walked around the grassy estate, sharing our views and ideas. She started out, I think, with legs, but by the end of the dream all she had was a head, which I carried with great tenderness and without alarm.

Awake and reflecting on this image, I am sickened—and a little afraid of myself. Then again, it was a pleasant dream, far better than one of my nightmares. I don't bother to ponder the meaning of a bodyless woman—I can't imagine a bigger waste of time than trying to analyze the bedlam of sleep.

As the first birds start chirping, Murphy gets to his feet, groans and stretches, then makes his way up to my pillow. While it is too dark to see his face, I know he can see mine. It's not like him to come up this close at this hour—maybe he had a strange dream of his own. What do cats dream? I know they do, I've seen their feet and whiskers twitching. Are they victorious in their sleep, or frustrated like us? If they are hunting birds, do they prance away with a mouthful of feathers, or do they run in endless slow motion, jump and continually miss?

I pet the warm furry span between Murphy's ears and he starts to purr, and this, for several minutes, is my world. How simple life is, lived in moments. How utterly safe.

The heat from Murphy's body is making me too warm and the back of my head is aching. I had too much wine, I realize, remembering the bottle I shared with Andre last night, the glass I poured, foolishly, when I got home. Rolling onto my side I open the window wider and lay back down, and Murphy calmly repositions himself alongside my ribs. Now I can feel the fog coming in; it seeps through the screen, falls on my face in cool tiny droplets.

Barbara. I look at the glowing red numbers on the alarm clock. 5:20, 8:20 her time. If I try right now I might be able to catch her before she leaves for work.

"C'mon, Murph," I whisper, getting out of bed. Slowly, stiffly, he gets to his feet and jumps to the floor with a thud. We cross through the kitchen and I open the door to let him out. Murphy maintains a regular schedule and always opts to relieve himself before breakfast. I don't know where he does this; he's a modest cat and conducts his business privately.

Cradling the phone under my chin I dial Barbara's number and start preparing my coffee. She answers so quickly that I am caught offguard and can't find my words.

"Hello?" she demands a second time.

"Hi Barb."

"Lorrie! Hi. I just hung up the phone, like two seconds ago."

"Are you busy?"

"No—I mean yes, but I have a few minutes." She is checking her watch, I know it.

"Listen," she says. "I talked to mom yesterday. She broke her arm."

"Jesus. How?"

"She slipped off the back steps and tried to catch herself."

"Is she okay? Is it a bad break?"

"She said it wasn't. They're going to take the cast off in four weeks and check it. It's her ulna—her forearm. I'm glad it's not her shoulder, she's had so much trouble with her shoulders."

I nod, trying to imagine my mother with a cast on her arm, lighting cigarettes, wrestling one-handed with an ice cube tray.

"How is she managing?" I say, opening my bag of French roast.

"Okay, she says, but everything takes twice as long. The hardest thing is getting in and out of the bathtub. I told her she should be taking sponge baths, and she said she tried that but hates not feeling clean—you know how she is."

"When did this happen?"

"Three days ago."

"Her right arm?"

"Oh yes," Barbara sighs. "*And* I talked to Bett. She said she wanted to talk to you too but you were working."

I light the burner and frown. "Damn it. I wish she'd call me in the morning."

"I think she'd been drinking," Barbara says, her voice lowered in disapproval. "She kept talking about Russell, how he really wasn't so bad, that he had a lot of good points."

Sure he did. Every time I think of that creep I get furious. The last thing I said to him was, "Please take care of my little sister." I didn't say it with a smile either. "Oh I will," he said, nodding and grinning, dumb as can be. Of course I didn't believe him—not that I imagined he would end up beating her.

"And then she told me she heard Gram one night. She heard her laughing."

This stops me. This is the sort of thing I'm afraid of.

"She says it's so quiet at night that she can hear things she's never heard before. She says she can feel things too, that she felt Russell walking beside her one day when she went down to the marina. Weird, huh?" I open my mouth to answer and Rita says, "Oh—and she's going to see a palm reader next week. She's real excited about that."

"She's leaving us," I murmur, more to myself than to Barbara.

"What?"

I stare at the water boiling in the saucepan, trying to understand what I just said.

"This world isn't working for her, Barb. She's trying to find one that is."

There is not enough tangible evidence in that remark to interest Barbara. "Hmmm," she says politely.

I take the pan off the stove, return to the facts. "Did she get that puppy? Some woman was giving away St. Bernard puppies."

"God I hope not," Barbara says. "She didn't mention it."

"Did she tell you about Rudy?"

"Oh yeah. Poor guy." She pauses, chuckles. "She says they're thinking of starting a bait shop. I guess Rudy has a couple old bathtubs in his yard, and a refrigerator, and she says they can raise crayfish and minnows in them."

Smiling, I wrap my hands around the warm coffee cup. Just as I'm about to comment on this, Barbara tells me she has to be going.

"But tell me," she says, "did you check out the jobs at the university?"

"I did," I say, relieved that I don't have to lie. "But there wasn't anything viable—I mean, there wasn't anything I was qualified for."

"Are you sure?" she says. "Did you talk to someone?"

"Well, no—I read the job board."

I can see her shaking her head. "You have to speak with someone," she says. "They probably don't post every job."

"I'll go back."

She says she'll call in a few days and apologizes for having to go and we say goodbye. It doesn't hurt to hang up the phone like it does with Bett; still I wanted to talk longer. I wanted to tell her more about Ginger. On second thought, maybe it's just as well I didn't. What I want to talk about she doesn't want to hear.

Rita knocks twice, then strides through the door and into my kitchen, filling the place with perfume and color. She is wearing gold earrings and a turquoise top that shows off her neck and shoulders, and she is radiant. In fact I can't help staring at her and wondering if, right here, right now, she has reached the zenith of her beauty. Does it happen that way? Does beauty, servant of time, unfold precisely? Is there a day, an hour, in which we are as lovely as we will ever be?

"Hi!" she says, hugging me too hard. Against my back I can feel the coldness of the food she is holding.

"Hi," I gasp.

She lets go of me and puts the groceries on the counter. "You look tired. Did you have a bad night?"

"No." I turn away, open a cupboard and take out another coffee cup. I'm a little annoyed, to tell the truth. I was just about to tell her how good she looked.

"I couldn't decide," she says. "I bought two kinds of melon." She pulls them out of the bag, a Casaba and a Crenshaw, then fills the counter with everything else she purchased: fresh blueberries, cream cheese, peppered lox, onion bagels and pulp-free orange juice.

"All my favorites," I note, not without tenderness. I'm not mad anymore.

"Is it ready?" she says, pointing to the coffee.

"Of course," I say, taking the carafe off the stove. "You know me."

We set the food on the coffee table—there is no other place to eat in this cottage, unless you want to stand at the butcher block in the kitchen. Rita takes a bite of her bagel and her eyes widen when she sees the the tankful of baby guppies.

"*Four* aquariums?"

"It's temporary. They're breeding so fast I had to set up the quarantine tank."

"What are you going to do with them?"

I look at the tank and sigh. "I guess I'll give them to a pet store. The adults too. I never should have bought them, I don't know why I did."

"Keep two females," Rita suggests. "A nice lesbian couple."

Grinning, I drape a lustrous slice of salmon on my bagel. "There's an idea."

Rita takes a sip of coffee, sets it down. "Okay," she says. "Tell me about Sharon. How did your date go?"

Sharon. I haven't given her a thought.

"It didn't go anywhere."

"What do you mean? Did you meet her?"

"Oh yeah." I cock my head, look at her in bewilderment. "Rita, haven't you noticed that freaky way she keeps smiling? At nothing?"

"No."

"I can't believe you haven't noticed that. She does it all the time, smiles and stops. I didn't know what the hell was going on. And she talks too much."

Rita crosses her arms over her chest, arches an eyebrow. "Anything else?"

"Isn't that enough?"

"No," she says, "it's not enough. Has it occurred to you that maybe she was nervous? You can be pretty intimidating, you know." I have heard this before and it baffles me. "Was there anything about her you liked? What about her looks—don't you think she's cute?"

I nod, shrug. "She's cute. Got a real cowgirl thing going." I reach for my coffee. "Does she dress that way all the time?"

Rita frowns.

"I'm just *asking*," I protest. "She looked good."

"I think you're getting eccentric," she says.

"That's not fair. You set me up on a blind date, it doesn't work, so I'm weird? Rita, *there was no spark*. End of story."

Rita takes a bite of her bagel, regards me doubtfully. "Don't you get lonely?"

"Yes," I tell her, "but it's not life threatening." I pluck a fat blueberry off my plate and pop it into my mouth. It is sweet and cool, and tastes, well, *blue*.

"What about you?" I ask. "How're things with Sheree?" I can see her discomfort immediately.

"Oh," she sighs, "I don't know. Not great, I guess." And she slides me an unmistakable look of guilt.

"Hah! There's someone else."

"We haven't done anything," she says, holding up both hands. "But yes, I have met someone. Her name is Georgia."

"How did you meet?"

"It was at one of those women in business things, a lunch in the city. That's where she lives."

"What does she do?"

Rita smiles, proud already. "She's a calligrapher."

And we start talking about Sheree and how she's always studying—she wants to be physical therapist—and when she's not studying, she's playing softball (Rita rolls her eyes at this and I nod in sympathy). They are running out of conversation, and the sex, Rita adds, is "becoming tragic."

"Is she unhappy too?" I ask.

"She has to be," Rita says, turning solemn. "Right?"

"Probably."

Rita puts her graceful fingers around the edge of her coffee cup and spins it slowly on the tabletop. Her pink lacquered nails are perfect as usual; I resist looking at my own.

"So what should I do?" she murmurs miserably.

I know Rita, at least I think I do. I know that she's smart and restless, that her love affairs usually last about a year and that our longevity was a misguided achievement. How nice that after all the drama she put me through, I can sit here like this, calm, amused, a little bit bored.

"The question's not *what*," I say, reaching for another berry, "but *when*."

After breakfast Rita and I go out back and sit in the deck chairs. Rubbing Murphy's neck and chin, Rita marvels over the marijuana ("I can't believe you're getting away with this again"), the vegetable garden and the lush sweet pea vines splashing the fence with red and purple flowers. She misses this yard, she tells me, and Joel—how is he? (She doesn't ask about Sasha.) He's fine, I tell her, happy and handsome.

"They're in Tahoe right now, I've got the place to myself." I roll up my sleeves and Rita notices my arm.

"Is that where you burned yourself?"

I look at the reddened area; the skin is smooth and shiny and doesn't feel like my own when I run my fingers across it. "Yeah. It's healing pretty fast."

"Must've hurt like hell," she remarks, crossing her legs and turning her face to the sun. She is wearing white capri pants and chic leather sandals and a pair of sunglasses with dark green mirror lenses; leaning back in her chaise longue she looks like an advertisement for the good life.

A large butterfly appears in the garden, a black swallowtail with yellow spots, and I hold my breath watching it dart among the sweet peas. Murphy notices it too, but knowing his limits he stays put.

I am just about to bring up the subject of Ginger when Rita says:

"Are you still seeing that little girl?"

I look over at her profile.

"Yes," I reply. "Against popular opinion."

There is a pause and I know that Rita has understood, that she will caution me no further.

"How is she?" she asks. "Are you still reading to her?"

"Oh yeah. We finished Black Beauty and she wanted more horse stories so now we're reading The Black Stallion. That reminds me." I sit up, face her. "Why are children's stories so grim? There's a horse in Black Beauty called Ginger—of course Ginger was all excited about that. Anyway, this horse has a terrible life and dies from cruelty. Think about it: Bambi, The Three Little Pigs. *Hansel and Gretel.* Fairy tales are the worst."

"You're right," Rita says, nodding. "They're awful."

I gaze at a velvety black bee that has just landed on one of the cosmos, bending its long thin stem. "As if kids aren't scared enough." And then, as a breeze ruffles the corn and Murphy idly licks his paw, I say:

"I think she's being abused. Sexually."

Rita turns her head and I see my reflection doubled in her sunglasses. "Why?"

"Because I spoke with her about it."

"And she said something?"

"No—that's just it. She wouldn't say a thing, wouldn't even look at me. I asked her and she went mute."

Rita lifts her hands, palms up, in a gesture of patient exasperation. "Maybe she had nothing to tell. Maybe you just scared her."

I say nothing to this and she continues. "Lorrie, have you ever thought about what your childhood might have done to you? Maybe you see—you're *prepared* to see—things that aren't there?"

I glare at her a moment, too mad to speak. I'd expect this sort of reaction from Barbara, but not from Rita, who, as a matter of fact, has a story or two of her own she'd rather not remember.

"Rita, how many women do you know who have been molested?"

The question hangs in the air until she leans back in her chair and sighs, "Plenty."

After that we talk about Ginger's parents. I tell Rita more about Shirley and the art class she's taking, and then I tell her about the garage, the tires piled in front of it, the brand new padlock, the black paint.

"I think he might have guns in there. I found a couple gun magazines in the livingroom—he's just the type to be selling them." I look at the sweet peas, innocently clinging to the fence. "He drives down to L.A. a lot. He's probably buying them there."

Rita shifts position, recrosses her legs. "Maybe he's selling that fake designer stuff. You know—jeans, purses."

I snort. "I doubt it. That's a little too sophisticated for him."

"He sounds awful," she says with a shudder. "What are you going to do?"

"I don't know yet. I'm not sure there's anything I can do."

Rita turns my way and nods firmly. "And remember, if he's arrested then Ginger will probably go into foster care. That could be a worse situation than what she has now."

I stare at her. "You think I haven't thought about that?" I say, my voice breaking. "I've thought about it plenty."

Her face softens with remorse. "I'm sorry, Lorrie. Really." We are quiet for a moment, and then, changing the subject, she says:

"I talked to my friend, the travel agent? She said the closest airport to where Bett lives is in Kingsport. It's in North Carolina, but it's right across the border. I guess you can probably take a bus from there," she adds, her voice doubtful.

I shake my head. "I don't think so, it's pretty rural."

"Can she pick you up? Maybe a friend can give her a ride."

I shrug. "Maybe."

"You know," she says, carefully, putting a hand on my arm, "if you ever wanted to get your license"—I glance at her, alarmed—"you can practice on my car. I'll take you driving anytime you want."

"Thank you," I say, touched that she is offering, and not for the first time, to put me behind the wheel of her cherished Mustang. "I'll think about it."

And I do, that very minute. I see it happening. Me, getting into a car, turning the key, driving down the road like anybody else.

Wouldn't it be something! I could knock on Bett's door like I'm borrowing some sugar; I could walk right into her kitchen, catch her sitting at the table. Oh to see the look on her face!

"Why do you call her Bett?" Rita asks. "Her real name's Elizabeth, right?"

I smile, remembering. "She couldn't pronounce it. She called herself 'Lizbet,' emphasis on the 'bet.'"

"That's cute," Rita says. "Liz*bet.*"

I start talking then about my conversation with Barbara and how worried I am about Bett.

"She's drinking again, for one thing."

"Oh no," says Rita, who knows about Bett and her binges.

"And she's imagining things—she said she heard our grandmother laughing." I swing my gaze back to Rita. "Remember what I told you about that counselor and what he said about Bett?"

Back when Bett was in junior high she had to meet with a counselor on account of something she'd said or done (I never learned the details) and the counselor told my mother that he was concerned about Bett, that she was displaying "delusional tendencies" and he thought she should be evaluated. My mother, who doesn't believe in personality disorders, or school counselors, ignored this, in the same way she had shunned other unpleasant facts.

"I remember," Rita frowns. "And I can't believe your mother didn't do anything—*all* of you should've had counseling."

I gaze at a black and blue mark on my kneecap and think about this. Would it have made any difference? What is the treatment for a child betrayed?

"You know," Rita says, engaged in her own speculations, "she had to have known—the showers he took with you, the naps. All those nights he went into your *room?*" She shakes her head, disgusted.

Suddenly I am pierced with an image, unaccountably vivid. My mother in her bath. Her legs look like sticks in the water; her arm, heavy in its cast, rests on the edge of the tub. I can see the pink tiled walls, the freckles on her shoulders, the thin green washcloth she is holding to her face.

Scars. Blame. We're all living with something.

FIFTEEN

Shirley doesn't like the art class. She says they make you draw everything in circles and she doesn't draw that way, and that the people are "stuck up." Also, you can't smoke and she draws better when she smokes. All this alarms me—I don't want to lose my private time with Ginger—and I grope for reassurances.

"First days are always hard," I tell her. "And I think there's a reason for making those circles; I think they make it easier to get the proportions right—you know, so you don't end up with the head being too big for the body."

Shirley taps her cigarette against the tire and scowls.

"And as far the people go, maybe you need to give them a chance. Maybe they're just shy."

She shakes her head knowingly. "They're not shy."

I don't know how to respond to this, nor do I know what to say about the smoking: that it's bad for her anyway? that the discipline will help? No. I am losing this argument.

"The money," I blurt. "You paid for the course (well, I did). You might as well get your money's worth."

I think she actually considers this, out of guilt, which is fine. Whatever keeps her in that class.

"I need another sketch pad," she says, crafting a bargain. "I used up a lot of pages. And another eraser."

Buying time with Ginger will be a lot more expensive than I thought.

Ginger is keyed up this morning, thrilled at the prospect of seeing the fire-works tonight. Rita asked me yesterday if I was going down to the marina to watch them; I hadn't even thought about it.

"Do you have to work?" she asked.

"No, the restaurant's closed."

She threw up her hands. "Then let's go! Sheree's housesitting for her mom this week, so I'm solo. Hey—maybe we can take Ginger. Why don't you ask her mother?"

So I did. Shirley is coming too; she says we can all ride together in the Galaxie. Won't Rita be surprised?

Most of the flowers have survived and I tell Ginger what a good job she did transplanting them.

"I water them every morning," she nods, and by the splashes of dirt on the cement I can see that she does.

"What's wrong with those?" she asks when I pull out a couple sagging mari-golds.

"Well, sometimes, if they're weak to begin with, the change is too much for them. It's called shock."

"Are they dead?"

"Pretty much."

"Maybe if we give them more water."

I shake my head regretfully. "It won't help."

"Oh!" she says suddenly. "The cat next door? It had *kittens*. I seen two of them. A black one and a stripey one."

"Saw. You *saw* them." It pains me to hear her speak this way and I correct her every time, quickly, as if I'm ridding her of evil, as if words, the right ones, might save her.

"My mother says I can't have one." She juts out her chin, summons a look of dejection. "Do you believe that? She says it'll make messes and she says I won't take care of it. I *will*," she declares.

I place my hand on her arm. "I know."

Her eyes widen. "Maybe you can tell her. Tell her that I'll feed it everyday. Oh! And it can stay in my room. Tell her I'll keep it in my room," she nods.

I'm wondering what shape those kittens are in. I can't imagine anyone in this neighborhood bothers with veterinary care. They'll need shots, de-worming, flea baths, ear mite medicine. Litter and a box. If I handled all that, and bought the food, would Shirley say yes?

Then I remember. Him.

"But what about your father?"

Immediately her face falls, she looks away. "He'll say no," she says, simply, and I am moved by her conviction, her pure and unassailable despair.

It's the perfect time to show her what I bought.

"I have a present for you," I tell her, opening my knapsack and pulling out the shoebox.

"A present?" she breathes, and reaches out her hands. I watch as she pulls up the lid, peeks inside. "Oh!" she cries.

They are sneakers, high-tops just like mine, only they're yellow. With rainbow laces.

In wonder she runs her finger along one of the laces.

"You can wear them tonight."

She looks up, beams at me, and I see Bett again. More than the glasses, more than the snarly blonde hair, the broad forehead, it is the mouth that unites them: the color and shape of the lips, that touching overbite. Is there really a link here, a clue, or is this just one of those incidental echoes, nature running out of room and overlapping itself? With all the people on this planet, I suppose it's not surprising that two might be given the same mouth.

Of course she wants to put her sneakers on now. We both look down at her grubby naked feet and I tell her she should wash them first, and put on socks. Just as Ginger yanks open the screen door Shirley comes out of the house.

"Hey! Slow down, will ya?"

Ginger holds up the box. "Look!"

"Hmm," Shirley says, eyeing the shoes, then me.

"I hope you don't mind," I tell her. "She really likes my red ones, so I bought her these."

Shirley pauses, gives a hard shrug. "I hope you didn't spend a lot of money—she'll grow out of them in a month."

"Nah-ah!" Ginger yells as she bounds into the house.

Shirley slides a look out onto the street, clears her throat.

"But, you know. Thanks."

She is wearing purple stretch pants and, although it's cool this morning, a tank top that shows off her cleavage, which I notice she has optimized with a dark smudge of make-up. I try to catch her eye but she avoids that, and seeing the goosebumps on her arms, the blue veins above her breasts, pity sweeps through me.

"You're welcome."

"I better get," she says, and nodding toward the door, "You can go inside, you know. *He's* not home."

I watch her walk across the yard and get into the Galaxie. '*He's* not home.' Shirley doesn't know how I feel about her husband. I guess it's no secret how much he hates me.

Ginger is perched on the side of the tub wiping her feet with a damp washcloth. On the floor beside her are her new sneakers and a pair of faded pink socks, the fabric thin and gray at the heels.

"Did you use soap?" I ask her.

She rolls her eyes dramatically and points at a cracked bar of soap sitting in a nest of bubbles. I hold up my hand and make a circle with my thumb and forefinger, indicating approval.

Two limp towels hang near the tub and Ginger yanks one off the rod and rubs it across the tops of her feet.

"I'll finish lacing these," I say as I squat down and pick up a sneaker.

Immediately she reaches for the shoe. "No! I can do it."

"Okay," I shrug.

I've used their bathroom a few times and it always looks about the same: there's a ring of scum in the tub, fuzzy grime around the base of the toilet and the trash is overflowing. I've seen worse. I'd like to check out the medicine cabinet again, see if there's anything new, but I can't do that with Ginger in the room, so I walk back into the hallway.

"I'll be out there," I tell her. "Take your time."

Passing Ginger's room I glance inside, noticing once again how spare and neat it is; except for the magazines pictures on the wall it could be a nun's room. It isn't likely that Shirley insists on these standards—what compels her daughter to be so tidy? Is she simply trying to make a pretty place in this ugly house, or is it safety she's after? Does she hope that by making her bed, stacking her books, she will keep harm away? It didn't work for me.

I look at the other door and imagine her father crossing the hall, entering this room at night. Because that's what they do. They come right in. They don't care that your room is supposed to be safe.

My stomach tightening, I walk over to the door and take a step inside. It smells of Shirley's perfume, sickening, like a giant, fetid gardenia, and beneath that another smell—unwashed laundry; there's a pile of it on the floor. His jeans are on top, the legs splayed in different directions. Something is sticking out of the pocket, a piece of paper, and I walk over and take it out. It's a list of names, all men, and phone numbers; below these is an address—someplace in Oakland. The writing is cramped and hard to read, and the tiny letters are somehow ominous: he took pains with this.

That's when I see myself in the mirror: a wide-eyed, gray-haired intruder going through someone's pockets. I shove the note back where it was and just as I'm about to turn and bolt I see something else: two small photos tucked in opposite corners of the mirror. I've seen only one other photograph in this house—a school picture of Ginger on the fridge—and I can't resist examining these.

The lower one is a snapshot of Ginger's father, probably still in his teens, and an older man—his father, I assume. They are both crouched on one knee and holding rifles. In his other hand, Ginger's father is gripping a dead duck by one leg. The field is brown, the trees bare and both men are looking at the camera without expression.

The question is: who placed it there? Was this Shirley's whim, the proud wife displaying a photo of her manly young husband? Or did he, out of love or nostalgia, put it here himself?

The other photo is of Ginger's parents, much younger, straddling a motorcycle. Her face is fuller and, arms around her man, she is laughing; she is almost pretty. He is grinning too. In jeans and a denim jacket, mustache and long hair, he looks like any other boy back then. I might have dated him myself.

Could I be wrong about him? Are my views, as Rita suggested, too warped to be useful? Maybe he isn't a monster at all, but just another hapless human, soured by his own mistakes.

What am I basing my suspicions on? A certain look? A tidy room? Or did I make up my mind sooner—the instant I saw Ginger's face?

The idea is disturbing, disorienting, and I pause at the dresser, woozy with self-doubt.

That's when I become aware of my leg pressed against the mattress. I have tried to avoid looking at their bed, but now, bracing myself, I scan the dented pillows and rumpled sheets, and I think of his skinny body stretched out there, and that scar on his stomach, and this time I really do bolt.

Shirley is driving, I'm riding shotgun and Rita and Ginger are getting acquainted in the backseat.

"I'm going to have a farm," Ginger is saying, "and I'm going to grow horses." She chuckles, clamps her hand over her mouth. "RAISE!" she says. "I'm going to raise them." I wink at her over the seat.

The traffic on Shattuck is worse than usual and Shirley's driving unnerves me. Elbow out the window she is steering one-handed and paying more attention to the people on the sidewalk than the cars in front of her; she gets too close, then brakes too hard. Twice now Rita and I have shared an anxious glance.

I feel a little bad about Rita, who, in new linen slacks and matching jacket, gamely climbed into this old car. There's a big rip in the upholstery beside her and it makes me wince to see her now, delicately pushing the foam back in. I'm sorry, I mouth, and she lifts a shoulder to show me she's fine.

Shirley holds up her pack of Kools. "You mind?"

Rita and I shake our heads no.

"Good." She punches the lighter and shoves a cigarette between her lips. As soon as the lighter pops out she grabs it, and I watch her eyes squint against the heat as she presses the red coil to the cigarette. The fresh smoke wafts my way; like a note from an old friend it gives me a wistful feeling. I quit smoking several years ago and while I don't crave cigarettes anymore, I do miss the fun we had.

Shirley drapes her arm over the seat; gratified by the nicotine, she's game for anything.

"So," she says, eyeing Rita in the rear view mirror. "You cut hair, huh?"

Rita sits forward, eager to please. "Yes. I have a salon on Vine Street."

"What do you charge?"

"It depends," Rita explains. "On what you want. I do styling, hennas—"

Shirley grabs a fistful of her red tangles. "Can you fix *this*?"

Rita's eyes widen. "Ah, we can talk about it. We can talk about your options."

"Well you can't cut it short, I know that. I made that mistake *one* time—Bill hates short hair."

The sound of his name works like a bomb, sending small shockwaves through the car. At that very moment we pass by the Mitchell Brothers cinema, Berkeley's pornographic movie house, and I glower at the marquis.

Ginger flips the door lock up and down. "I wish Margarita could come with us," she sighs.

I look sideways at Shirley and see her eyes crimp; that's where pain lives, in the hollows around our eyes. Shirley never talks about Margarita and now I know why.

I start babbling about firecrackers and how they were invented by the Chinese, but they weren't really firecrackers back then, they were just pieces of bamboo that exploded as they burned. In no time at all I have bored everyone, including myself, and when Shirley makes a sharp right turn and bumps us against the curb, I take it as a warning.

Dusk is an hour away but already the marina is packed with people. For several minutes we wander through the throng, stepping between blankets and trying to find a patch of grass big enough for the four of us. We settle for a narrow strip alongside some people wearing turbans and they nod their heads in a formal greeting. On the other side of us is a family of Asians, a tired-looking husband, a wife who won't stop talking to him, a teenaged boy with Downs syndrome and two girls about Ginger's age who might be twins.

As soon as we spread out our blanket and sit down Shirley lights a cigarette and starts searching the crowd, her head darting this way and that. We don't matter now; she didn't wear her shiny purple pants and heart-shaped earrings for the likes of us. Ginger, meanwhile, is watching the Downs Syndrome boy. He is sitting cross-legged, rocking from side to side and smiling to himself. At least they have that, I think. At least they were given their own fount of joy.

"Shirley!" someone yells and we all look in that direction. A chunky woman in a tight black top is waving madly and Shirley springs to her feet. "My friends," she says, pointing with her thumb, trying not to show us how thrilled she is. "Guess I'll go say hi." Rita and I watch as she stumbles over neighboring blankets and happily approaches her own kind, a rowdy trio sprawled around the biggest cooler I've ever seen. One of them is a man with a full beard and tattoos down both arms and Shirley pokes him with her foot by way of greeting. I didn't know she had any friends, and how astonishing that she should find them here, just four blankets away.

"I brought brownies," I announce, pulling a foil package out of my backpack.

Rita looks over at Ginger and whispers, "She makes the best brownies in the world. She makes them with caramel."

Ginger exaggerates a look of amazement, opening her mouth too wide and bugging her eyes. Palm up, she extends her hand and I place two small brownies in it, a star and a circle. I do, as a matter of fact, make the best brownies in the world, and Ginger eats hers slowly, letting the soft brown caramel ooze out onto her fingers, which she licks with total absorption.

A chilly wind kicks up and we all put on the jackets we've brought. Ginger's is too big, naturally, and there's a large stain—it looks like oil—on the pocket. I haven't seen one of these jackets in years: dull green fabric with a floppy hood and a furry orange liner. I help Ginger with the zipper and then we all lean back and look at the indigo sky and the first stars of the evening.

"Do you know what that one's called?" Rita asks, pointing to the brightest star. Ginger shakes her head.

"Venus."

"Oh," Ginger cries, "Oh! That's number two!"

Rita beams at her. "That's right. Venus is the second planet from the sun."

"Mrs. Beck taught us the planets," Ginger explains. "Saturn has rings around it." She looks over at the twins to see if they're listening: they are, their heads turned at precisely the same angle, like a pair of young foxes. "And Jupiter," she says, getting haughty, "has two—"

A boom resounds and everyone turns and looks out over the bay where red, white and blue streamers arc and fall.

"Ooh," Ginger breathes. She scoots over then, settles in the V of my legs with her back against my chest. I am so surprised by this spontaneous affection that for a moment I don't move. Across the blanket Rita arches an eyebrow and smiles, and I sit up and carefully bring my arms around Ginger's small frame. That's how we watch the fireworks: her hands squeezing my knees, my chin just touching the top of her head. It's a good show, lasting nearly an hour, and everyone cheers when the finale lights up the sky with neon spirals and golden cascades.

Shirley shows up right after that, flushed and grinning, and I know she's had a couple beers. I don't begrudge her the drinking, but I am annoyed that she didn't watch the fireworks with us, didn't care, apparently, about witnessing her daughter's delight; and to make matters worse, she doesn't even apologize; I don't think it even occurs to her. That's how it always is with Shirley: one minute she's melting my heart, the next she's giving me chills.

Nobody says much on the way home. It takes forever to get across town and Shirley is very close to nodding off when we pull into the driveway. Her face is harshly illuminated by the light over the garage: she looks old. There is something very sad right now about those heart-shaped earrings, which jiggle as she shoves the gear shift into park. She looks over, catches me watching her, and immediately her expression changes, the exhaustion giving way to worry. She's afraid I don't like her anymore. She's made me mad and she doesn't know what to do.

Well I have an idea.

We all get out of the Galaxie and say our goodnights in the yard. Rita hurries to her Mustang (she wasn't thrilled about leaving it here) while Ginger, with a mournful wave, trudges into the house. Shirley turns and starts up the steps and I reach out a hand to stop her.

"Um, Shirley? I wanted to ask you about something. I'd like to take Ginger to the Steinhart Aquarium."

She looks at me blankly.

"It's in San Francisco."

Still no glimmer of recognition.

"She'd love it," I explain. "And you can come too," I add, "if you want."

She shifts her weight, squints at me. "What is it? What do they have there?"

I open my arms wide. "Everything. Great big tanks, every fish you can imagine. Sharks, octopus. Sting rays."

"Yuck," she says, making a face. "Go ahead. But I'm not going—I hate fish."

SIXTEEN

The guppies are gone. I ran an ad in the Express and gave them to the first person who called, a middle-aged black woman with impeccable manners. She sets up aquariums in elementary schools, she told me, and is always in need of fish, particularly the easy ones. She commented on how many guppies I'd raised, and how beautiful some of the males were, and she was surprised that I didn't want to keep any of them. I just shrugged and handed her the warm plastic bags of fish, which she gently tucked into a box. I did consider keeping a couple females, as Rita suggested, but the thought dismays me—two lone females, the last of their species, swimming round and round in baffled, barren silence.

Now, sipping my morning coffee and peering at the tanks, I notice that the one of the platys is pregnant. This business just can't be stopped.

Joel is the backyard; I can hear him singing Sloop John B, one of his favorites.

"—around that old town we did roam—"

Nassau town—he never gets that right. Setting down my coffee cup I walk over to the window and see him snipping leaves off the pot plants. His hair is longer these days and he's growing a mustache, and when he glances over at me and smiles, he reminds me of a cowboy. A gorgeous one.

"Hi!" he says, "C'mon out." He puts his fingers to his lips, inviting me to share a joint.

"I have to make a phone call first."

"No problem," he says with a wave of his scissors. He turns back to the plants, starts singing again.

Behind me Murphy is busy scratching his neck with his hind foot.

"C'mon, buddy." He follows me into the kitchen and meows faintly when he sees me take the fleacomb off the window ledge. I think he likes this ritual, to a point, because he always purrs when I begin; but after a couple minutes he squirms away, as if the pleasure is too great, as if he doesn't deserve it.

After that I head for the fridge and pull out the orange juice and a tray of ice cubes; then I pull the vodka out of the cupboard and make myself a screwdriver, which I drink in the kitchen while examining my houseplants. In these long hours of sunlight they're growing more readily: the sweet potato vine is twining around the window; even the date palm looks like it has a future.

Back on the sofa, I finish my screwdriver and eye the telephone. Maybe someday I'll be able to make this call stone cold sober. Maybe not. It's not so much for courage, this drink; it's more for protection. A supplemental layer of skin.

Taking a deep breath, I pick up the phone, dial the number.

"Hello?" she asks in that familiar wary tone.

"Hi, mom. Barbara told me about your arm."

Juan has disappeared again (this happened twice last year). We assume he's in Mexico, but he could also be passed out on somebody's sofa right here in town. It doesn't much matter and nobody will ask. He'll walk into the kitchen in a few days, visibly shaken by whatever he went through, and without a word to anyone he'll start scraping plates, and we will all avert our eyes and pretend that nothing happened, because that's how we apologize for giving him a life he hates. That's the bargain.

In his place tonight is a scared-looking Hispanic boy named Arturo who is trying very hard to do well. Nimble as a rodent he scurries out of my way, and every time I use a bowl or cutting board he grabs it and hurries to the sink. "Donde?" he keeps asking, holding up sheet pans and rubber spatulas, and I point him in the right direction with my chef's knife.

Ann bangs one of the swinging doors open.

"The oil needs to be changed," she announces.

I don't look up.

"Now," she adds.

The door swings back and the dishwasher looks over at me, puzzled, smiling, ready to help. Apparently I'm supposed to be the translator.

Ann's in another foul mood; she's blaming her period. When she came in today she told me that she was "hemorrhaging" and that the last place she wanted to be was "this goddamn pit."

Zee, who's standing at the pantry table juicing lemons, says, "I'll show him."

I look over at her and smile my thanks.

"You're too good, Zee. What am I going to do without you?" Soon she'll be leaving us again, for three long months, and like always I'm going to miss her terribly—and not just because Suzanne will be her replacement. Which reminds me, I have to talk to Molly: there's no way I can work with Suzanne again.

"Oh, you'll manage," she says, wiping her hands on her apron and giving me a pat on the shoulder as she walks by.

And I will, that's the thing. I'll keep on cleaving chicken and slicing up squid and yanking the beards off mussels and throwing out slimy chunks of tuna and burning my arms on the oven racks and smelling like all the fish and fowl and beasts I've handled. It's easier than you can imagine. One day, for fun, you tie on an apron and five years later you notice it's still there.

I roll the beef tenderloin over and slip the tip of my knife under the silver skin. How many of these have I trimmed? Lewis told me that the hormones get through your skin, that little by little your body absorbs whatever they're giving the cows these days. Am I going to grow hair in new places? Will my nails start to thicken? Nobody knows yet.

So guess what happens when Arturo changes the deep fryer oil? The inevitable. Zee shows him how to drain the old oil and swab out the crusty bits of squid and onion, and that goes fine. The trouble comes when he hoists the tub of new oil and pours it into the fryer—without putting the drain plug back in. I come out to the bar for a club soda and there he is on his hands and knees trying to mop up a spreading sea of FryMax, using every last dirty towel and napkin we had in the hamper, while Ann, arms folded across her chest, looks on in disgust.

I take my soda out back and sit on an overturned bucket and look up at the cedars, their tops moving in the high breeze, so far from where I am. I came out here to clear my mind, but that doesn't happen—it never does. I'm thinking about the puttanesca sauce I have to make, and if we have any capers, and if I can salvage any of the tomatoes that are rotting away in the storeroom.

There's a rustle in the dumpster beside me. I turn my head and see a rat calmly climbing out of the rubbish. He teeters a second on the edge and we behold each other with mild surprise before he drops to the asphalt and saunters into the ivy.

I swig down the rest of my soda and rub a patch of dried beef blood off my wrist, and then, like always, I go back into the kitchen. What will it take to stop me?

This is my fourth time driving Rita's Mustang. I've managed the streets okay, and even the curves on Grizzly peak, and now Rita's giving me some tips on backing up and parking. We're in a church parking lot on a Monday morning, so I have lots of room for error. One hand on the wheel, the other gripping the back of the seat, I am looking behind me as we travel the length of the lot in reverse.

"That's right," she says. "Nice and easy. Don't over-steer."

I give a slight nod and concentrate harder. Rita is a good teacher, patient and encouraging. In fact she used to be a teacher's assistant before she started cutting hair. We reach the far curb and she says, "I think you've got it down. You want to do some parallel parking?"

My heart thuds. "Do I have to? Is it on the test?"

She shrugs. "I don't think so. But still, you should learn. Sooner or later you'll need to do it."

For the next half hour I drive up alongside a perfectly innocent Volvo and try to end up squarely behind it. After a few dozen tries I succeed, but only because I've finally chanced on the right angle. Rita, knowing this, congratulates me anyway.

"You want to do it one more time?" she asks.

Sweaty, arms trembling from the effort, I shake my head.

"Okay." She pats my thigh. "Wednesday we'll go on the highway. You're doing great," she tells me again. "Have you thought about what kind of car you want?"

I look at her in disbelief. "Rita, I can't think about that yet. All I can think about is passing the test."

"Oh for god's sake—of course you're going to pass." (This is another one of her teaching tactics: visualizing success.) I pull out onto Sacramento Street, and she says, "Maybe we can find you a used Mustang."

I tell her I'd love to get a Mustang, but what does she think about Hondas? They're supposed to be very reliable, aren't they? Good mileage and all that? After all, I am going 3000 miles. And they're probably cheaper than Mustangs. Rita considers this and says that's true, but Mustangs are fast, which means they're safer on the freeway; you can pass in a wink. And there's a whole lot of freeway between here and Virginia.

Rita has some things she wants to talk about, so we decide to have lunch at a place just off Telegraph Avenue that has a second story deck, great pizza and a view of the campus. The waitress, a young woman with short black hair, appears at our table and I count the small silver rings in her ear (seven) while she takes our order.

Rita spills her silverware out of the napkin. "I broke up with Sheree yesterday."

"Oh?" I didn't realize it would happen this soon. "How did she take it?"

"Not very well. She wants me to have all my 'shit' out by tomorrow."

"Did she cry or just get mad?"

"Both. A lot of both."

I gaze at the Campanile tower in the distance and picture Sheree's face, reddened with tears and wrath. I've never had much feeling, one way or another, for Sheree, but she has my sympathy now.

"Look," Rita says, pointing at a faint lipstick print on her wine glass. We both grimace.

"Where are you going to go?" I ask.

"My sister's, til I find my own place. Georgia offered me her apartment, but that's a little premature. And anyway, I think I need to stop moving in with my lovers."

Lovers.

"So you've slept with Georgia?"

Shamefaced, she looks at me askance. "Saturday night was the first time. It was"—she breathes in, shakes her head in wonderment—"incredible."

Naturally. "What does she look like?"

Rita settles her chin on her hand, taking pleasure in the evocation.

"Well, she's short, like you, and she has long brown hair that she wears in a braid. She's got great muscle tone—she works out with weights. And she likes to dance, and she's passionate. *Very*," she adds, raising an eyebrow for emphasis.

Okay, that's all I want to know. I mumble something about looking forward to meeting this woman, and then I start talking about Ginger and a funny thing she said.

"I told her about loggerhead sea turtles and how they swim hundreds of miles through the ocean to lay their eggs on the beaches where they were born. I told her that no one knows for sure how they find these beaches and last week she told me her theory. She said they follow the sound of the music. She said that the sand sings to them."

Rita smiles. "That's cute. She's a cute kid. Smart, too."

I beam as if Ginger is mine. "She is, isn't she?"

Rita's face changes, becomes serious. "But she does seem young for her age. Her speech patterns, her mannerisms."

"Yeah?"

Rita nods. "I used to work with that age group. Eight-year olds are very out-going, very chatty and social. Ginger's more withdrawn."

"She is," I agree. "She keeps to herself; I've never seen her playing with other kids."

"She's a worrier," Rita says. "The way she fiddles with her hair, those knots."

"I know. I wish I could get her to stop doing that."

The waitress comes with our pizza and salads. Rita shows her the lipstick smudge on the wineglass and she gives us a embarrassed apology and hurries down back down the stairs to fetch a new glass.

"Okay," I whisper. "Now take that fake cockroach out of your purse."

Rita laughs. "You're confusing me with one of your seedy friends."

The pizza looks inviting: strips of roasted red bell pepper, onions, artichoke hearts, black olives and goat cheese. I pick up my fork and start in on the salad, a delicate heap of organic greens with yellow tomato wedges.

"Oh. Shirley's not going to anymore art classes."

"That was fast—how many did she attend?"

"Four."

"Why is she quitting?"

"She says the people are mean and that she isn't learning anything."

The waitress comes back with a new glass and the carafe of white wine we ordered, and I pause while she pours it.

"Also, she wouldn't admit it, but I think she was missing the reading sessions—she likes to listen when I read to Ginger."

"Do you mind her being there?"

I shrug. "It's not the end of the world, but now I can't get anymore one on one time with Ginger. It's harder to connect with her when Shirley's there. She's...inhibiting, and she needs a lot of attention—more than Ginger."

Rita pulls a triangle of pizza from the plate and hot trails of cheese follow. "Well, school starts next month and pretty soon you won't have much one on one time with Ginger anyway."

I frown and pick up my glass. "Yeah, I know. We'll have to get together on the weekends. I guess."

As if reading my thoughts, Rita says, "What about her father? Is he home on the weekends?"

"I don't know when the hell he's there. I've only seen him a couple times. It's so weird the way he comes and goes—Shirley doesn't seem to mind at all."

Rita, chewing her pizza, nods. "She probably likes it that he's gone a lot."

A bus goes by and the exhaust rises up to greet us. On the street below a stream of young people flow in and out of a record store. Lurking in front of the dry cleaners next door is a man I recognize. Thomas Havenot. He's famous around here. What he likes to do is spring out in front of people and scream at them. Twice he has targeted me, his eyes red and wild, his neck veins bulging. "I'm going to kill you," he roars. The police can do nothing. He's too healthy to be hospitalized, too crazy to be prosecuted.

"When did you say you're going to the Steinhart?" Rita asks.

I brighten at this, straighten up in my chair. "The Monday after next. Did you want to come?"

"I can't. And besides, this is your day, yours and Ginger's."

"You know, she's never even been on BART? We're going to make a day of it: the aquarium, lunch at Pier 39, a trolley ride—the works. Next time I want to take her Lake Anza so she can go swimming."

Rita lifts her wineglass and studies me, her expression thoughtful. She opens her mouth, about to tell me something, but I look her right in the eye and she changes her mind.

"She'll love that," she says, and reaches for another slice of pizza.

I'm making my bed and watching news clips from the LiveAid concert—Tina Turner with her savage hair; Mick Jagger hopping around in tight pants—when Bett calls. I turn off the volume and settle back against the pillows, and for several minutes Bett amuses me with colorful anecdotes about life in Burkes Pond. There's a bar in town, she tells me, that she and Rudy go to sometimes. It has a handwritten sign on the door that says, Open 7 am til 10 pm—if folks don't stay. I have a good laugh about this and she goes on to tell me about Jesse and Luke. The bar doesn't doesn't bring in much money, she says, so when the rent is due each month Jesse and Luke come in and drink whatever is owed.

"You're making this stuff up," I say, wiping tears from my eyes, and she assures me she isn't. A couples seconds go by and I hear her light a cigarette.

"I wish you were here," she says. "I got fired."

"Why? What happened?"

"Oh this asshole was being mean to his kid. Lorrie, this kid was like six years old and this guy whacks him, right on his temple, just because he couldn't figure out how to buckle his life vest. So I called him a few names and they fired me." She breathes out a stream of smoke. "I don't care. I hate that place."

"What are you going to do—for work, I mean."

"Oh, I can get a job. Rudy got a new truck—well it's not new. Rudy's brother died and he left Rudy his truck and his guns." Bett coughs, clears her throat, and I frown into the receiver: I wish she wouldn't smoke. "Anyway, it's a lot better than Rudy's old Ford, which isn't even running right now, so we can work in Quincy. There's plenty of jobs there."

"Rudy's looking for work too?"

"Yeah. He's not making enough on disability."

"What about the bait business?"

"What? Oh. We're not going to do that right now. There's not much fishing after September. The refrigerator leaks anyway, we can't use it."

Murphy looks at me for permission, then jumps up on the bed and politely curls himself into a fat gold ball. Bett asks what's new with me and I tell her about my own job and how much I'm beginning to despise it.

"It's a dog's life, Bett. People think we wear nice clean uniforms and pipe out little pastries, and it's nothing like that. It's hard, dirty work—and the pay sucks."

"So quit," she says in that dead center way of hers.

I give a sigh and pet Murphy, whose face is hidden in his stomach. "Yeah. I know I need to. Barbara thinks so too."

"Oh. I called her last night. Jonathan's been acting up in school."

"What's he doing?"

"Backtalking the teacher. Showing off. I think it's because of Barbara—you know how she pushes those kids. Jonathan's probably just trying to get back at her."

"Maybe." I think of Barbara and her regal beauty, how tall and straight she stands; how much she asks of herself, how much she wants for others. Wherever it came from, anger or unspeakable hurt, she forged that iron will of hers, in private and long ago.

"Oh," says Bett. "She's having some tests done. Her stomach, I think."

Alarmed, I sit right up. "Why? What's wrong?"

"Well, you know, she didn't really go into detail. She just said she was having some problems. She thinks it might be a flare-up from when she got sick in Mexico."

"That was like two years ago!"

"Lorrie," Bett says, "she's *fine*. God, you're such a worry wart." I hear the click of her lighter again, an exhalation of smoke. "Oh—that palm reader I went to? Her name's Freida. She's amazing. She knew so much about me. She even knew about Russell and the accident."

I'm wondering how Freida got this information, whom she bribed or tricked. Rudy probably.

"She told me I'm going to live on a beach someday and I'm going to meet a man with two first names. And she says I'm going to have a child, a little girl."

"Hmmm." I want to thrash this woman.

"She says I was a war widow, and that my husband was killed at Gettysburg." A pause. "You know, one time I dreamed about a soldier. He was wearing a gray uniform—that was the south, right? Frieda said we lived in a white mansion."

I can't listen to anymore of this.

"That's interesting," I remark, and then, before she can answer, "Hey—do you remember Ginger, that girl I told you about?"

"Yeah. That little kid who looks like me."

"Yep. I'm still reading to her, a couple days a week. We just started Justin Morgan Had a Horse—wasn't that one of your favorites?"

"Little Bub!" she cries. "Oh, I loved that story." Leave it to Bett to remember the horse's name. I've never known anyone with a memory as exhaustive as hers.

Suddenly she is sad. "I wish you could read to *me*," she says. "I have all these books and I don't even read them. I start them, and I just, I don't know, I start thinking about other things…"

I wait, my hand strangling the receiver, and I hear her sigh.

"I want to play Boat. I told Rudy about it. I tried to play it with him, but he didn't get it. Nobody does, just you. Don't you miss Boat?" Her voice is nearly a whisper.

I was going to tell her about taking Ginger to the Steinhart, but I've changed my mind.

"Bett. Are you okay?"

"Yeah," she says, her voice faraway and reluctant.

"Do you need any money?"

Predictably she says no. "I don't have to pay rent next month cause I'm going to put a new roof on the cabin."

"A roof? You know how to do that?"

"Rudy's going to help. He says it's really easy. Oh!" she cries. "I'm getting some kittens on Friday. Two for sure but maybe five."

"Five!"

"Lorraine? She runs the post office. Her cat had kittens and if they're not adopted by this weekend her husband said he was going to bring them to the pound in Quincy, but that's a lie. I know he's just going to drown them, so I'm going to take them."

"You're amazing, you know that?"

"I know!" she says, and I can see her grinning. "Hey, I'd better go now."

"Are you calling from Rudy's?"

"Mm-hm."

"Where's he?"

"Picking beans in the garden."

"What are you going to do now?"

"I have to clean up my kitchen. You should see it," she chuckles.

"And then what?"

"God Lorrie, I don't know. I guess I'll sit down and have a beer."

It's easier, being left with something, to say goodbye, and for several minutes after we hang up I stay where I am and picture Bett sitting at her kitchen table, gazing at some Queen Anne's Lace just outside the back door. There, poised on the tiny white flowers, is a butterfly, its sky blue wings opening and closing, opening and closing.

We're together once again: Ginger and me on the sofa, Shirley hunched over her sketchpad, listening to the story I'm reading. Apparently all these children's books are new to her and she follows each one almost as closely as Ginger does. I've encouraged her to read them to Ginger herself, in the evenings or whenever, but this doesn't interest her. She says it's more fun with me and that I'm a better reader anyway. "I can't do those, you know, all those voices and things."

Today she made us lunch again—hot dogs and Kraft macaroni and cheese, red licorice sticks for dessert. She cut the hotdogs into small pieces and stabbed them with frilled toothpicks; the licorice she presented in a yellow-striped drinking glass. It was a festive event.

All Ginger can talk about is our trip to the aquarium. I told her we're going to ride a train that goes under the water and one that goes straight up to the sky, and she started waving her arms and hopping around the livingroom. She is in charge of the food, I said: ordering our soft pretzels and choosing where we're going to eat lunch.

Maybe I shouldn't take all the credit, but I think she's happier now than she was a few weeks ago. She talks more, and gestures exuberantly, and lately she gets into those helpless giggle fits that children succumb to. She is a worried child—she will be a worried adult—but there are times when she is free of that, when she is lost in what's left of her childhood: riding black stallions, swimming with sea turtles. How soon before that world retreats? What will I offer her then?

Today's visit ends abruptly, at the sound of a truck pulling into the driveway. Ginger hunches up; once again she hides her hands between the sofa cushions, a response that disturbs me. Shirley grinds out her cigarette, slaps shut the sketchpad—does he disapprove of her drawing as well?

"That's Bill," she says needlessly.

Braced for his entrance we all look at the door. He doesn't appear right away and after a moment I say I need to leave, that I have to get an early start on my prep for tonight. Shirley knows I'm lying, but I can tell she's relieved. I give Ginger's knobby knee a pat and from behind her smudged glasses she looks at me anxiously.

"See you next time, kiddo." I get to my feet. "And thanks for the lunch, Shirley—it was great."

She gives me a nod and looks back at the door.

His truck is there—even that looks menacing—but I don't see him until I am halfway across the yard. He is standing at the side of garage, turning the key in the padlock; on the ground at his feet are two large cardboard boxes. His dark hair is slicked back from his face; he is thin as a knife. The sight of me startles him and he lets go of the padlock. Instantly his eyes narrow, his mouth twists. I think about Ginger, her hands shoved into the sofa. I was going to offer a greeting, a meaningless hello, but an old rage seizes me and I do something stupid: I glare right back at him; I give him a look he can't mistake. Then I turn my back on him and walk away.

There's no question. I have lost.

SEVENTEEN

"Lorrie?"

I recognize that rough voice immediately—and I want to hang up.

"Yes?"

"It's Shirley."

I force a slow breath out.

"Hi," I say, trying for a tone of pleasant surprise.

"I got your number from that order, you know—that make-up you ordered? You're not in the phonebook."

"No. My number isn't listed." I've never been in a phonebook, not in any of the places I've lived. I don't recall my reason for this; now it's just a habit.

Seconds pass. She clears her throat. "Bill? He wanted me to call you."

My stomach tightens, I feel sick.

"He...um..." She struggles for tact, gives up. "He don't want you to come by anymore."

I knew what she was going to say, but I can't think how to respond. I reach for the sofa, steady myself. Nothing in the room seems real.

"Why?" I manage to ask. It's a pointless question and I'm not surprised when she doesn't answer.

"What about the aquarium—I promised her."

"No," she says, so quickly that I know he must have threatened her about it. "You can't do that. Bill don't want you taking her anywhere."

"What about you?" I cry, angrier at her than at him. "What do *you* want? What about Ginger?"

I can see her frowning. This is too much for her; any second she's going to hang up.

"It's not right," she says, "you coming here all the time to see Ginger. I'm her mother. You're not even related."

Cornered, confused, she's using his words now. It's no use, she won't help me. I never gained any ground at all.

You can't depend on the mothers, I should know that by now. Other mammals protect their young with their lives; I have yet to encounter that trait in our species.

"I thought you liked me coming over," I say, futilely. "I thought we were friends."

A pause. Then, in a rush, she says: "Look, I gotta go. Thanks for reading those books to Ginger, but you can't come here anymore."

"Shirley!"

"What?"

"I can't...I mean, what'll she think if I just stop coming? I need to say good-bye at least."

She doesn't answer.

"Can I just come over and do that? Just for a few minutes?"

She waits, sighs. "Yeah. Okay. But not tomorrow. Come on Friday—he won't be here."

I thank her and we hang up. I'm so grateful for this small favor that several seconds pass before I realize what I have asked for.

"I don't know what to say to her," I tell Joel.

We're in the backyard facing one another. Beside us are the marijuana plants, taller now than I am. It's a cool morning, still foggy, and Joel, who's been working on a new mural, is wearing a gray sweatshirt spattered with blue paint; I can see more specks on his tanned cheeks and forehead.

I have just told him about Shirley's phone call. I know he can't give me any answers but I look into his eyes and ask him anyway:

"What am I going to tell her?"

He shakes his head and puts his arms around me, and that's of course when I fall apart. Who knows how long I stay there, my head against his shoulder, breathing in the mingled odors of laundry soap and fresh paint.

I awake, breathless, from another bad dream. I was running on a country road and two faceless men in a car were chasing me. My legs were getting heavy and I started slowing down, and then the road turned slick and muddy and an immense chasm opened on my right. I had to run carefully so I wouldn't slip off the edge, but of course I did and that's when I woke up, the sheets twisted round me, my pajamas damp with sweat.

Some cultures believe that the body is protected by the soul. During sleep, they say, the soul can escape and when it does we dream.

Anything can happen to us in our sleep, which is why children fear it. No use trying to comfort them: they know their dreams are real.

When I arrive at Ginger's house on Friday morning the Galaxie isn't in the driveway. That coward Shirley has ducked out on me.

This time Ginger isn't waiting on the porch steps; she's standing next to the garage, peering at the roof. She is wearing her purple dress and, as usual, her yellow sneakers. So intent she is on whatever is up there that I'm just a few feet away before she notices me.

"Listen!" she cries, rushing over and grabbing my arm. "There's a kitty in the garage!"

I wait a few seconds and sure enough I hear a small and bewildered meow.

"I think it got in through there," she says, pointing to a gap in the rotted wood. Just beneath that is a dead branch from a large plum tree. The kitten must have jumped from the branch and into the hole, and now it can't find its way out.

"I've been calling and calling," she tells me, "but it won't come out." She turns her worried face to me and the sunlight flashes across her glasses. "I think it fell a long ways."

For several minutes we try to coax the cat out of the hole; each time it answers with a pitiful cry.

"This isn't working," I mutter, frowning at the stacks of tires, the locked slide bolts. Abruptly I walk around to the side door and eye the new padlock, and Ginger, following me, says:

"I seen where he puts the key."

I turn and gape at her.

"There," she says and points to a crumbling row of bricks along the garage. I squat down and turn over the first one, disturbing several earwigs. I try the one beside it and uncover nothing.

"It's the next one," Ginger urges. I lift the third brick and there it is: a shiny, dangerous treasure. I hesitate a second, then pluck it from the gray dirt.

"Where's your mom?" I ask.

Ginger shrugs. "She said she had to go someplace. She said I can't leave the yard. She says that if you come over we can't go *any*where." She frowns at me. "Do you *believe* that?"

"Yeah," I tell her. "I do." I face the door's black painted window, and, heart pounding, I grasp the heavy padlock, push in the key and turn. With a smooth click the lock pops open.

I can't find a switch near the door but there's enough light coming in for me to see a string pull hanging from the ceiling. I walk over and click it on, and the brightness of the naked bulb startles me. The air is dank; long gray cobwebs hang from the corners of the room; I smell mold, motor oil, turpentine. The kitten cries again and Ginger and I look over at the shelf it's hunkered on, a good four feet below the hole near the ceiling. Beneath the shelf are piles of electronic equipment, stereos mostly, and lots of cardboard boxes.

"Oh," Ginger cries. "There it is!"

I cross the room, climb up on a box and reach for the kitten, who hisses and backs up.

"He's scared," Ginger whispers.

I put my foot on another box, crushing the top but gaining another couple inches, and nab the kitten by the back of its neck. It struggles frantically but calms down when I'm back on the floor and holding it to my chest. It's a grey striped kitten, lanky and underfed; gazing at my face with great interest it starts to purr.

"Oh, oh! Can I hold it?" says Ginger, reaching up. I slide the kitten into her hands, feeling its ribs against my fingers; she brings it close to her body and kisses the top of its head. I start to stop her—who knows what this animal might be harboring—then change my mind. Let her love what she can.

While Ginger coos over the kitten I lift the lid on a long box next to my feet, uncovering, just as I suspected, a glistening rifle, one of those weapons with a handle to hang onto so you can keep shooting. I open another box and find a large television, still encased in its packing material. The creep has sure been busy.

A few rusted shovels and rakes lean against the opposite wall, along with a push mower and a small charcoal grill, both shrouded in cobwebs. Next to them is a work bench piled with tools, paint cans and solvents; nails and screws are scattered on the cement below.

There is something in the corner hidden beneath a large green tarp. With a glance at Ginger, who is talking earnestly to the kitten, I walk over and pull back the edge of the tarp, revealing two large boxes. I step closer, open the cardboard on the first box and uncover a hoard of videotapes; there must be over a hundred of them. In the other box are two video cameras; one of them looks brand new. None of the tapes are factory labeled, though many are stickered with a date. They are not stacked in order and rummaging through them, I find dates ranging from April 6, 1982 to July 25, 1985—barely a week ago. Without a second's pause I snatch two of the tapes—the most recent one and another near the bottom that doesn't have a sticker—and shove them into my backpack.

An engine roars up the driveway and I am flooded with terror. Ginger, gripping the kitten, jerks her head toward me. She opens her mouth but is too frightened to speak. This is not Shirley's Galaxie, this is a truck.

We stare at each other, waiting for the engine to stop, a door to slam. I will kill him. I will kill him if he lays a hand on her.

But we are saved. Whoever it was pulls back down the driveway and rumbles off. The kitten cries, bewildered. I hear Ginger let out her breath.

"Let's get out of here," I say, yanking off the light and grabbing her hand.

It's a sunny morning and the air is laced with the scent of the ocean. How indifferent, how heartless the weather can be, offering such splendor on a day like this.

I was going to tell her the truth, that her father has forbidden me to visit. But then I thought how awful that would be for her: she fears him now, shall I make her hate him too? I wonder what he thinks I will tell her. I doubt if he cares.

"Is that where the kittens live?" I ask Ginger, pointing to the house next door. She nods.

"Do you want to take their kitty back to them?" Ginger hesitates and I add, "I'm sure they'll be happy to see it."

"Okay," she sighs. The kitten, getting restless, starts to squirm. Gripping it more firmly she walks across their lawn (it's yellowed in some spots but at least they have one) and up the steps to the front door. Watching her from behind— those small hunched shoulders—I blink back sudden tears. A few seconds after she rings the bell a robust Hispanic woman appears at the door. "It got in our garage," I hear Ginger explain, and the woman puts her hands on her wide hips and shakes her head at the kitten, feigning annoyance, then smiles hugely and lifts the cat from Ginger's arms. "Gracias, mija," she says, tousling Ginger's hair, and I understand that she knows Ginger and is fond of her. It's a pleasant surprise; I guess I assumed that no one here cares about anything. Looking at the yard more closely I see the efforts they've made: the daisies planted along both sides of the front walk, the Christmas lights stretched over the porch, the pair of plastic fawns lying under a squat palm tree. I move my gaze to Ginger's yard, a dirt square edged with dead shrubs, stained with circles of oil, then back to the fawns and daisies, and I am struck by the requisite balance: for every sign of neglect in this world, there must be an answering show of faith. How else would we survive?

She is going to have a farm, Ginger tells me as we're sitting down on her porch steps (I will not go inside that house today, even for a minute), and she's going to have lots and lots of kittens, *and* horses. I tell her I think that's a fine idea, that there are not enough homes for all the animals in the world.

"Maybe," I suggest, "you can get a job rescuing animals. Not just kittens; you can rescue all kinds of animals—ducks, squirrels, baby bunnies."

"I know," she says. "That's what I'm *going* to do."

I unzip my backpack and start taking out the books I've brought her, almost my whole collection, as many as I could carry.

She picks up James and the Giant Peach and tilts her head at the cover.

"That's about a boy who takes a ride in a peach."

She looks at me quizzically. "How can he fit inside a peach?"

"You'll have to read it and find out." I place another book in her hands. "Have you ever read Poppy?"

She shakes her head.

"It's about a mouse and an owl—you'll love that story."

I pull out the last of the books and nudge the pile toward her. "You can have these. You can read them whenever you want."

She studies the illustration on the cover of Poppy; I watch her run a finger over the mouse's tail.

Behind us are the two clay pots we planted; they look good, the flowers have grown.

"You have a green thumb," I tell her. Immediately she looks at her thumbs.

"It's just an expression," I laugh. "It means you're good at growing plants."

"I grew a sunflower for Mrs. Beck," she declares, "from a seed. I grew it in class."

We talk for a couple minutes about sunflowers and why they're called sunflowers, and then there is an empty space, a signal to say what I came here to say.

Trying for a light, brisk tone, I tell that my schedule has changed, that I have to work more hours now and I can't come over and read anymore, at least for a while. Before she can ask, I tell her that we can't go to the aquarium either—not yet. I almost add, wildly, that the aquarium is closed for repairs, but decency stops me.

"Later on," I say, avoiding her eyes, "we'll go sometime later on." This is really not a lie; I believe it.

Ginger doesn't. When I finally look up to meet her gaze, she is staring at some point in the street, rolling the hem of her dress between her fingers.

"Ginger."

She turns. Her face is remote, almost calm, the hurt stowed away. If she were older she would give me a last look of contempt and walk away. But she doesn't know these stratagems yet. Unaware that she can wound in turn, she is simply waiting for me to leave. Her acquiescence appalls me. How long has she been expecting this moment?

"I'll be sending you some pictures in the mail," I tell her. "Pictures from magazines. Letters too."

She nods politely, looks at her feet; I realize she thinks I'm lying.

I sit there a few more minutes, trying, with no apparent success, to offer something in the way of encouragement, words that will serve as gifts. At one point I tell her how smart she is; I actually grasp her thin arms and turn her toward me, trying to make her understand that she can do anything in this world, *any*thing, and she regards me with distant wonder.

After I hug her—she allows me this—I start to cry. Not wanting her to see this, I pick up my backpack and hurry down the steps. This time when I get to the end of the street I don't look back. It would be awful either way: if she were watching or if she weren't.

In the shaded streets of my neighborhood life goes on: flitting birds, dozing cats; people moving behind rippled windows, reaching for books, opening cupboards. One of them waves, startling me. Out of habit I stop in front of the yard that's filled with birdfeeders, not the kind you buy in stores; these are homemade versions, fashioned from plastic bottles, cookie tins, egg cartons, even grapefruit halves. They hang from the redwood trees and from hooks under the eaves; some are perched on tall wooden stands. Usually I stay for several minutes watching the sparrows and finches hopping from feeder to feeder, but today I lean on the fence and look at nothing. I'm thinking about Grizzly Peak, where Rita and I went driving yesterday, and how nice it would be if Ginger's father were to fall off one of those stony mountainsides and die.

I just read an article about that. This husband and wife were traveling at night through Utah, the canyonlands, and the wife had to relieve herself. She got out of the car, squatted on the side of the road—then oops, over she went. Lost her footing, or so he said. He added that she'd had a couple drinks at a bar beforehand (I think he was padding the story at that point). The beauty of this crime is, who can dispute it? No bullets, no knife, just one little shove.

It got me wondering about all those vacations that people take to the Grand Canyon. Of course there are options all over the world. For something charmingly British, you could take your spouse to the white cliffs of Dover; for a more adventurous excursion you could visit Central America, nudge your hubby off a Mayan temple.

Harder when the person you want to get rid of is just an acquaintance, someone you have no ready access to. How would I lure Ginger's father up on Grizzly Peak? And what if he didn't die? What if I just maimed him?

If only he could manage it himself. Drive into a tree like Russell did. There's hope, I suppose. Maybe on one of those long drives down to LA he'll take a curve too fast; maybe a trucker, dozing off for just an instant, will swerve into his lane.

There's a squirrel staring at me. He is perched on a redwood branch just a few feet from my head munching on something between his paws. A point of light glints in his shiny brown eye and under the scrutiny of this small bright animal, fully engaged in being what he is, I feel exposed, foolish, piteously human, stuck for the whole of my life in a wheel of useless thoughts.

When I get home there's a message from Rita on my answering machine; she has some information for me on childhood education classes.

We talked about this yesterday, when I was telling her that I had to find a way to see Ginger, that even if I couldn't go on reading to her I had to keep in touch with her.

"Why don't you get a job at her school?" Rita said. "You could be a teacher's assistant. You'd only need to take three or four classes for that; it wouldn't take any time at all.

"If you like it, you could get into the teaching program at the university. Have you ever thought about getting your teaching credentials?"

I shook my head. "I couldn't do that, Rita. All those kids, year after year. Kids that come from homes like Ginger's—or worse. Seeing all that hurt, all that damage—"

Rita broke in then, she was angry. "Stop looking at it that way! You look at everything that way. Does it hurt less if you turn your back on it? Why not *help?* Give comfort, make them feel loved."

I blinked at her.

"Look what you're doing now," she added. "That's better? You hate cooking."

And then, knowing I'm sensitive about it, she finished up with this:

"You have a degree. Use it."

I'm sitting on the sofa, halfway through my glass of wine, when I remember the videotapes in my backpack. I don't have a VCR; I'll have to use Joel's.

Probably they're illegal copies. But of what? I can't imagine he's selling Hollywood movies. Maybe they have something to do with guns, survivalist stuff. Oh god—I hope they're not about animals. Traps. Poaching. Cockfights.

Some at least he's involved in the production of, or supplying the equipment. That really gives me the creeps, the cameras. And the dates.

Joel and Sasha aren't home but I have a key to their place and permission to come in anytime and watch their TV, which is four times the size of mine. As usual their bedroom is in cheerful disarray, with clothes and books strewn about, the bed unmade and inviting. On the wall above the dresser Connie Young, crouched over her bicycle, speeds past a cheering crowd.

I turn on the television and push in the first tape, the one dated July 25. Right away I can tell it's homemade. The camera keeps jerking and the voices are distorted. Sometimes you can hear, sometimes you can't. There's a man leading two children, a boy and a girl, down a hallway; they enter a room—it's just a room, it could be anywhere—and with slow horror I understand what is happening. The boy looks about seven years old, the girl is younger.

I take it out and, hands shaking, put in the second tape, the one without a date. This one is worse, not because of what they're doing, but because it's foreign. They are in some kind of shed. The man speaks to the child in what I think is Czechoslovakian. She is perhaps five years old.

I turn off the television, stare at the blank screen. I try to breathe.

Rita comes over right away. She doesn't want to see the tapes, doesn't need any proof. We just get in her car and drive to the nearest police station. The officer I talk to is very calm. She takes the tapes from me and puts them in a plastic bag, and then she asks me questions, so many that I start to get confused. Towards the end it seems like she's accusing me. What was I doing at their house, with their child? Why was I in their garage? And how did I get in if it was locked? And why did I take the tapes? Am I married? Do I have children? How long have I been at my job?

They need a warrant, she tells me. That usually takes two to three days. Apparently they have to make sure I'm not some kind of nut.

I ask her what will happen, what the police will do. She looks at me as if I'm dimwitted. They will confiscate the tapes of course, and any other illegal goods.

They will arrest the father, possibly the mother. Child Protective Services will arrange for temporary foster care for Ginger unless a suitable, and willing, relative can be located.

No. There is no chance she'll be allowed to stay with me.

EIGHTEEN

Bett has sent me a picture of herself, the first I've seen in years. She is sitting on a porch, three kittens in her lap, two wrestling beside her, and she is grinning at the camera. I can't help but grin back.

The smile is the only thing that hasn't changed. Her hair, dyed dark brown, is cut very short and her face is narrower. Her legs are long and skinny; there's a bruise on her shin. Though Bett was never what you'd call plump, she was by no means thin, and the photograph shocks me. She has gotten older, I hadn't considered that.

In her hand is a glass with something brown in it—bourbon, I suppose, her drink of choice. Her nails are short and painted red. There's an ashtray beside her with a cigarette in it. She is getting by.

Time takes people away from you. What I know about Bett, what I remember, now amounts to less than what I don't know. Still, I have the feeling that it accounts for something important, this private store of memories. I am her sister; she was entrusted to me. I shouldn't have let her drift so far. I should know what she has become, the gestures she makes, the way she walks, the way she laughs. It feels dangerous, not knowing these things.

There is a note with the picture, written in that same loopy style, the letters rounded and pushed together. "I've named them after the dwarfs—Sleepy, Bashful, Sneezey, Dopy and Grumpy. Love you!! By! XOXO Bett" With all the reading she used to do, you'd think she'd be a better speller. Details, though, she's never had much use for them.

I know that the bad stuff catches up with Bett, but maybe her world, on the whole, is easier than mine. Maybe it's preferable.

We spoke only once about what he did to us. It was in Little Rock. I asked her how she dealt with it, all those awful memories. She said, "Lorrie, I don't remember. I mean, I remember that he came into our room and took off his bathrobe and put it on the bedpost, but that's all. I don't remember what he did to me."

I was stunned. To not remember. To be able to not remember.

When I was in college my psychology professor once told me that there are two kinds of people in this world, those who escape and those who can't.

Several days pass before I remember the matchbook I found in Ginger's livingroom. I unzip the front pocket of my backpack and there it is, wedged inside a datebook I never use. Disturbing to think I've been carrying around a porn shop advertisement.

What if Big Willy's has been buying those videotapes? I think of that man speaking Czech, of rooms like that all over the world.

The note I found. The names and phone numbers he'd written down so carefully. I wish I'd taken that.

It was in the paper of course. William Douglas Hebert, age 33, and Shirley Moss Hebert, age 31, were arrested at their home on August 6. In addition to the videotapes, approximately $30,000 of stolen merchandise was seized. An anonymous tip led police to the scene. An eight-year-old daughter, Ginger Hebert, was placed in protective custody.

The police officer wants me to come down right away. She wants to see the matchbook. And she has a few more questions.

In light of my new familiarity with the local police Joel has harvested the marijuana plants a month early and is drying them at a friend's house. He has been wonderful through all this, but the real surprise is Sasha, who has knocked on my door twice this week just to see if I'm okay.

I think about Ginger all the time. The Child Protective Services has been very nice; they've made arrangements for me to visit her next week. She is staying, they tell me, with an elderly couple in Albany who specialize in caring for children in these urgent situations. In addition to this, she is receiving counseling. And yes, she has asked about me, several times.

How comforting it is to get acquainted with this hidden network, to see the good, to know that there are people out there quietly picking up the pieces, taking on the muck and misdeeds of others.

Shirley was released and is staying with her parents in Lodi until the trial gets underway. Ginger's father will likely remain where he is. My hatred for him is a huge dark wave that keeps coming.

They have asked me many questions about Ginger, her clothes, her diet. Have I ever seen any bruises on her? What has she told me about her father? How well do I know the mother?

Besides what the CPS discovers in their own investigations, Shirley may be denied custody of Ginger based on other things. Even if she is found innocent of any crimes associated with the items in the garage, a judge may decide that she *should* have known what was in there.

Sentencing a person for what she should have known. Is that really the purview of a judge? Isn't that a punishment we hand ourselves?

I look again at the picture of my mother sitting in a deckchair, hiding behind her sunglasses.

I remember the day perfectly. I had spent the morning happily catching minnows in one of the golf course ponds. I'd found a dead frog floating in the reeds and was using its ragged green carcass as bait. It was easy with the frog, the minnows swarmed right in. If I lowered my bucket into the water very slowly, I could pull in a dozen at a time. At some point I must have figured I had enough and, switching the sloshing bucket from hand to hand, I walked back home. The minnows were silver with rainbow sides. I was anxious to show them to my mother.

I set the bucket in the driveway and hurried through the back door. As soon as I came into the kitchen I knew that something bad had happened. My mother was sitting at the table—she looked awful; Barbara was standing a few feet away. Bett, in her thick glasses, her blonde hair wisping every which way, was hunched over the table. There was a book in her hands but she wasn't reading it.

"Come here," said my mother in an oddly quiet voice. I approached her cautiously, stopped when I reached the opposite side of the table.

"I want you to tell me something and I want you to tell me the truth."

They were all looking at me now. My heart was beating too fast.

"Your father," she began. Out of the corner of my eye I saw Barbara nod at me, very slightly. She was the one; she had done the telling.

My mother asked me only one question. Yes was all I had to say.

I'll never ask what it was, revelation or confirmation, but my mother put her face in her hands then and started to sob. That's when my life fell through me, there was nothing there at all. If I uttered a word, moved too quickly, I would disappear.

No one stopped me when I walked out of the kitchen and through the utility room to the back door. It was better outside; I still felt hollow but the terror had lifted, had become something else, something absolute and urgent. What I had to do was very clear.

I picked up the bucket of minnows—I didn't even look at them—and walked down my driveway, down my street, all the way down to the golf course. As soon as I reached the edge of the pond I poured the fish back into it. I was not the person who had caught them. I didn't know who I was, what world I was in, only that the minnows were not a part of it.

I feel that way now, compelled to get things done, as if my life has restructured itself and only needs my cooperation.

Rita wasn't surprised when I passed my driving test—she should have been: I hyperventilated twice on the way to the DMV. Afterwards, when I was too grateful, too shaken, too elated, too bewildered, to drive out of the parking lot, she stared at me in amazement, which goes to show you just how much she doesn't know about me. Not that it's her fault: who knows anyone? Deceit, lust, boredom, fear—marvelous how much we can hide.

I'm going to buy Zee's car, a dark blue '79 Toyota Celica with low mileage. She doesn't drive enough, she says, to justify keeping it, and she and Tom need some extra money to carry them through the next three months they'll be off. Joel has checked out the engine; everyone tells me it's a good buy, a nice-looking car. I've driven it a couple times, felt the plush seats, plugged in a tape, but so far I haven't felt anything I'd call pride. To me it's just a way to get to Bett.

I feel a new kinship with Zee; now both of us are on our way out. Ann keeps giving me suspicious looks but I know better than to share my hope with her. Zee's the only one who knows about the courses I'm going to take, morning classes that won't interfere with my work schedule. Rita still has a friend or two in the public school system and says she'll make some calls when I have all the units I need.

I'm going to give it a try, see if I can bear all those eager young faces. If I can start looking at them straight on.

I asked one of the social workers at the CPS about being a guardian, how to apply for that, and he gave me an armload of pamphlets, said it wasn't easy for a single woman to qualify. He knew it was Ginger I was talking about and he told me the chances were slim, that she had several aunts and uncles who were already being interviewed.

But there are other children, he added, many many others, and several options within the system for helping them.

Someday, maybe, but I can't take on those children right away. I need to start slowly. With playgrounds and storybooks.

"That's great!" says Barbara. "When do you start classes?"

"It's too late for fall enrollment, so I'm starting in January."

"I'm really glad to hear it," she says.

"I know you are."

"Can you live on those wages, though?"

"Tell you the truth, it won't be much less than I'm making now. But if I have to, I'll work part-time doing something else."

"You can always get your teaching credentials," she says, as I knew she would. "That would pay a lot more, and you'd get all the benefits. Hold on—let me take my earrings out."

I hear one, then the other clatter faintly on her countertop.

"Okay. You know, I never pictured you as a teacher. I never thought you liked kids all that much."

"I guess I was just afraid of them."

"Do you ever wish you had had a child?"

"I wouldn't go that far," I laugh. "How are your two doing? Jonathan still getting into trouble at school?"

"Oh no. Once we took away TV privileges and horseback riding, he straightened right up. He can't stand it when Alison is doing something he's not. Oh. She has a new passion—she wants to be an Olympic diver. I've lost some sleep over that, believe me."

"How's your stomach?"

"My colon, actually. Oh you know, they're not sure. They think it's colitis. They put me on steroids for a couple weeks and that helped."

I feel my eyes widen. "Steroids? It must have been pretty bad. Have you lost weight?"

"Lorrie. It's nothing, I'm fine." Deftly she changes the subject, starts telling me about a trip to Washington DC they're planning: the White House, the Capitol Building, the Lincoln Memorial, Arlington Cemetery. "I think the kids should see those things, don't you?" Absolutely, I tell her.

"You know," I say, "I'm taking a little trip of my own. I'll be gone for a couple weeks; Rita's going to housesit for me." Beside me Murphy rouses, looks up at my face; you can't tell me this cat doesn't understand what I say.

"What kind of trip?"

"A road trip. I'm leaving in two weeks. Everybody says that mid-September is a great time to travel."

"A road trip? Oh that's right! You're a driver now. So where are you going?"

"I'm going to visit Bett."

"Oh my god! You're going to drive that far? Alone?"

"Yeah," I nod. "I am. Don't worry—I won't be sleeping in the car or anything. I'm going to stay in motels."

"Have you told Bett?"

"That's the best part—I'm going to surprise her."

Barbara sighs. "Oh Lorrie, she'll be so thrilled. I wish I could see her face."

I grin. "I'll tell you all about it."

"You'd better. You'd better call me as soon as you get there."

"I will, soon as I find a phone."

She asks about Ginger (I have told her everything) and I say we had a very nice visit, that the couple taking care of her are wonderful.

"Helen and Keith. They're both retired professors. Nice home. Artwork, lots of books."

"Still," Barbara says, "it must be hard for Ginger. To be taken from her home like that. Does she miss her mother. Does she ask about her?"

"I don't know," I tell her, "she didn't ask me any questions about Shirley or her father. I think she's enjoying all the attention she's getting. Helen and Keith dote on her. And how about this—we're all going to the Steinhart Aquarium next week. I promised Ginger that I'd take her there someday."

"I'm so glad they're letting you visit her, Lorrie. I'm sure it helps Ginger."

I know she had a lot of misgiving about my attachment to Ginger and this remark moves me. That's the way Barbara is. She always comes up with the right words, the perfect gesture. After I told her about the tapes, how horrible that day had been, she sent me flowers. Something beautiful.

She asks if they've set a date yet for the trial and I say no, that the investigation is probably going to take a long time, and then she asks if it'll be hard for me and I say it will, it'll be awful.

"Do you want me to come" she says, "when you have to testify?"

I shake my head; I will not put her through that.

"No. Let's see each other when it's all over. You know…maybe I can fly back east for Christmas."

"That would be great! We just re-did the guestroom—you'll love it."

"Do you think we can get mom to come?"

"I just called her a couple days ago; I wanted to hear how her arm's healing. She said it's fine, just stiff. Anyway, she was complaining about the cold weather coming. What does it get down to where she is—55? I don't know if we can get her to come here in the middle of winter. Besides, you know how she hates to travel."

"Yeah, I know. But we need to work out something, next summer maybe. I've been thinking about her a lot lately."

I have to be going, I tell Barbara—my shift starts in 15 minutes.

"Please take care of yourself," I say. "I know you exercise like a madwoman and you eat all the right things, but you need to sit down once in a while, you know?"

Barbara laughs. "Yeah, I will. You too. You be careful on your trip. Do you have a route mapped out?"

"Yes, Barbara."

"Well, don't try to drive more than seven hours a day. And don't stay in any motels you don't feel good about. And call me. Call me along the way."

I've made it to Fallon, Nevada, my first stopover on the road to Bett. I thought about going a little farther, but I am woozy with exhaustion and my hands are cramped from holding the steering wheel so hard. The worst part was getting out of the bay area, dodging cars, getting sandwiched between semis, trying to find the right turn-offs. At one point, zipping past the exit I needed, I ended up in that V-shaped wedge that you're never ever supposed to be in.

After I crossed into Nevada, it was fine. The roads are so flat and empty here; no one seems to care what rules you break or how fast you go. It's a strange, woebegone place.

Barbara would not approve of the motel I picked, a low-slung pink building with 12 rooms and a tar roof, but I couldn't afford the Best Western down the street. Number 8, the unit I'm in, has red carpeting, a kelly green bedspread and a picture of crashing waves, an odd choice for a desert motel. It's not a terrible room but I don't want to spend anymore time in it than I have to.

Which is why I'm sitting in the Silver Lizard, a bar I found a block away. I like it here. It's exactly what you want and expect from a bar: cozy darkness, jukebox in the corner, all those bottles looking so cheerful: Chartreuse, Grenadine, Creme de Menthe.

I've spend the last half hour talking to a former Las Vegas showgirl who just went to the ladies room. She must be in her sixties, but she's holding up pretty well—you can tell she made her living off her looks. She is telling me about the casinos, what they were like, what it was to be a showgirl in the 40s. She seems happy enough now, smoking Virginia Slims, drinking Manhattans, and I think she probably had a very good life and that sitting on a bar stool in Fallon, Nevada is not such a bad way to end up.

There's a Hamm's beer sign on the wall behind the bar; I keep going back to it, falling into it. It's one of those electric ones, outlined in yellow neon, with a bright blue lake that seems to be moving and a bear in a boat paddling across. Bett would love that sign. I imagine her looking at it at night, when she's in bed and the room is dark.

I don't how much they'll charge me, I don't know if it's even for sale. I catch the bartender's eye, motion him over.

I'm not leaving this town without that sign.

978-0-595-36651-4
0-595-36651-1

Printed in the United States
58678LVS00004B/190-216